Th

Third Rider

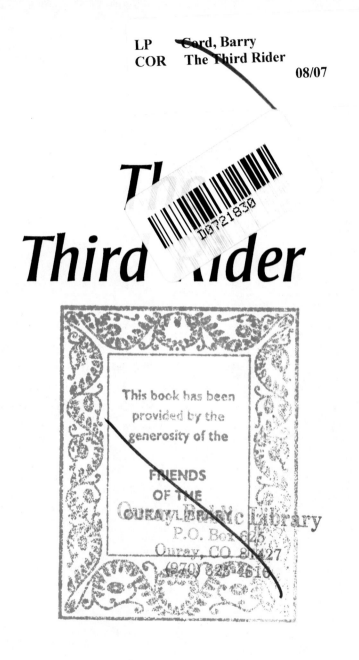

The
Third Rider

Barry Cord

WHEELER
CHIVERS

This Large Print edition is published by Wheeler Publishing, Waterville, Maine USA and by BBC Audiobooks Ltd, Bath, England.

Published in 2006 in the U.S. by arrangement with Golden West Literary Agency.

Published in 2006 in the U.K. by arrangement with Golden West Literary Agency.

U.S. Softcover	1-59722-224-0	(Western)
U.K. Hardcover 10:	1 4056 3751 X	(Chivers Large Print)
U.K. Hardcover 13:	978 1 405 63751 0	
U.K. Softcover 10:	1 4056 3752 8	(Camden Large Print)
U.K. Softcover 13:	978 1 405 63752 7	

The text of this Large Print edition is unabridged.
Other aspects of the book may vary from the original edition.

Set in 16 pt. Plantin by Elena Picard.

Printed in the United States on permanent paper.

British Library Cataloguing-in-Publication Data available

Library of Congress Cataloging-in-Publication Data

Cord, Barry, 1913–
     The third rider / by Barry Cord.
         p. cm. — (Wheeler Publishing large print westerns)
     ISBN 1-59722-224-0 (lg. print : sc : alk. paper)
     1. Cattle stealing — Fiction. 2. Revenge — Fiction.
     3. Large type books. I. Title. II. Wheeler large print western
     series.
     PS3505.O6646T58 2006
     813'.54—dc22   2006002248

To My Wife
Without whose faith this book
might not have been written.

Chapter I

Soso Creek seemed smaller in the fading
daylight, and the old split-rail fence still ran
a staggered line up the cedar slope, in spots
sagging inward, as if conscious of the
creeping desert sand pushing northward,
encroaching a little more each year on
Stirrup.

Mel Rawlins rode through a break in the
fence and reined his tired chestnut to a
halt in the middle of the ranch yard. The
weight of things long gone pressed against
the stillness. Then the barn door creaked
on rusted hinges and an old, slight woman
came out, an egg basket hooked over her
arm.

He waited, holding back an aching lone-
liness. The woman closed the door and,
turning, started at seeing a rider in the
yard. She stood very still, and the silence
of the evening lay between them — and the
changes five years had made in each of
them.

He saw no immediate recognition in her sun-wrinkled eyes. Looking at her, he caught the tightening of her lips, and he though dismally: *Have I changed that much?*

He forced casualness into his voice. "Evening, Ma."

She lifted her head, and a little tremor went through her. In the dying day she looked older, but there was the stiff pride in the set of her narrow shoulders which he remembered. She stood looking up at him, not speaking.

"You going to ask me in?"

She looked him over, searching that hard, dusty frame, seeming to look deep into Mel's dark, stubbled face to find the boy she had known, the baby she had labored to deliver.

"Come in, son."

He swung down from the saddle, feeling mute in her presence now, he who had been so harsh in his rebellion, so cocksure in his anger. She turned away without another word, as though he had just come in from riding fence with his father and his brothers — as though it weren't five years since he had had his violent quarrel with his father and left.

The ranch looked windswept and barren

as he put his back to the chestnut's flank and had a look around. Even the tall poplars his father had planted as a windbreak for the vegetable garden had a dusty, dilapidated look. The big corral was in need of repair, and he noted with no surprise that less than a handful of horses were being held within it.

He led the chestnut gelding to the water tank under the rock ledge by the barn. He let the animal drink; then he stripped saddle and blankets from it and turned the tired bronc into the corral and went into the barn for feed.

Chickens clucked at him from the darkness. He found no grain, but there was a half-bale of hay in the corner, and he brought out a couple of forks full and tossed them over the corral bars for the chestnut.

He came out and looked toward the house. A light brightened the porch windows. He put his long searching glance on the cane-bottomed chair on the veranda; it faced the low buttes to the south. His father had liked to come out and sit here at sunset and watch the desert buttes turn purple. The empty chair seemed mutely questioning.

Mel still had trouble believing what he

saw. Stirrup had been a big ranch, and some hard men had ridden for it.

He walked slowly across the yard. He could hear his mother moving about in the house, and he guessed she was setting the supper table; he thought he heard another voice, but it was faint and he could not make it out.

He stopped on the wide gallery to have a final look at the place.

This was Stirrup. His father had grazed a thousand head on the range behind the creek. Good range, running without a fence for almost fifty miles, clear up to the high plateaus of New Mexico on the northwest and the foothills of the Mogollons on the east. The desert lay to the south — a natural barrier — and Monte Rawlins had built his home here, because he liked the desert.

The irony of it struck Monte's oldest son now. For it was the desert that had beaten Monte. The desert and *El Patrone*. . . .

He raised his head, suddenly aware of vibrations in the stillness. He had lived with danger a long time; he had developed the cat-eyed instinct of instant alertness.

The riders came along the trail from town, shadowy against the shaggy poplars. They came into the yard and turned to the iron tank where the tiny spill from the rusting pipe made its quiet sound. They dismounted and let their animals drink a moment, then tied them to the corral bars and turned toward the house.

Mel saw that one was a woman in riding clothes. The other, lanky and with a slouched bearing, had a star on his unbuttoned vest.

Mel waited, frowning slightly. He had had his brushes with the law and he was not on easy terms with it.

They came toward the veranda just as his mother called from inside the house, "What's keeping you, Mel?"

The girl stopped, as though the twilight had suddenly thickened and imposed a barrier between her and the man on the porch. Mel saw her face in the dusk, round and soft, but with the direct glance and the stubborn chin of the Rawlinses. And the thought came to him that his sister had filled out as a woman and put on some extra weight, too. But then, Marilyn had never been thin. . . .

"Mel?"

Her voice held a mixture of reproof and questioning. The man with her put a hand on her arm and lifted a long, young face. His hat sat back on tawny hair, and there was toughness to the slant of his jaw, and a rawhide hardness to his lanky body.

Mel shifted slightly and smiled. "It's been a long time, Marilyn. I almost didn't recognize you."

"You've changed, too." There was neither anger nor pleasure in her voice, only the fading edge of surprise. She took a deep breath and turned to the man with her. "My brother Mel, Jim." And now a vein of bitterness sharpened her tone. "The prodigal son returns."

The lawman put his hard glance on Mel; his eyes measured the tall man with professional judgment.

"I've waited three years to meet you," he stated coldly, and started up the stairs.

Marilyn put out a hand to stop him, but he brushed it aside. He came up deliberately, and Mel squared away, not understanding the man's motives, but instinctively knowing what was coming.

"I promised Bob I'd do this for him," the man muttered grimly. He unbuckled his gunbelt and draped it over the railing. Turning, he feinted a left to Mel's stomach and crossed a hard right that caught Mel high on the cheek.

Marilyn stood at the foot of the stairs, her face whitening in the dusk. Her hands were clenched, but she made no sound.

Mel fell back against the house and shook his head and caught the next blows on his covering arms. A vicious belt to the stomach doubled him, and the lawman's knee, coming up, brought blood from his nose and put stinging tears in his eyes.

And then all the violence that lay within this man broke loose.

He came out of his crouch swinging, and he kept swinging, making no effort to defend himself. He was a little heavier than the lawman, and stronger. Mel slammed him hard against the side of the house, and his mother's startled outcry was lost on him. He kept swinging tirelessly for the man's face, stomach, face, stomach — backing him toward the end of the porch. The lawman staggered and tripped over the wicker chair, twisted away and came up holding it in front of him as a shield. Then he jammed it into Mel's face and followed it with a head butt that split Mel's chin.

Mel cuffed him around and slammed a hard right to the lawman's jaw that spun him completely around. A final slogging flurry dropped him to his knees. There was a stubborn will in this man that kept him trying. He was out on his knees, yet he tried to get up.

Mel hooked his fingers under the lawman's collar and dragged him to the steps and sent him tumbling at his sister's feet.

He stood above her, unaware that the door had opened behind him and that his mother was framed in the light it revealed. Marilyn stood over the beaten man, who was still trying to get on his feet.

"Nice company you keep, sis!" Mel said. His voice was ragged. He dragged in air and brushed blood from his chin. He felt battered and shaken, but there was an edge of respect in his tone as he said: "Maybe you can tell me what he was trying to prove?"

"A woman couldn't keep better company," Marilyn said. Her voice held a stiff pride. "Jim's my husband!"

She bent over him now, laying gentle hands on his shoulders, restraining him from crawling up the steps. She wiped his bloody face with a handkerchief.

"You tried, Jim," she said softly. "Bob couldn't ask for more."

Mel stood there, trying to put things together, trying to find the answer to the puzzle, and hearing an inner, bitter voice ask him why he had come back!

Hump's letter, reaching him at just the right moment, when he was at loose ends and a bit tired of looking over the next hill?

A man should never look into a mirror after a bad night, he thought. *It makes him feel sorry for himself, makes him vulnerable.*

Marilyn lifted her face to him. "Why did you have to come back?" Her voice was dull, bitter.

Behind Mel his mother's voice was sharp. "That was uncalled for, Marilyn!"

The girl stood stiffly at the foot of the stairs.

Mel said slowly: "I didn't start it, sis. I didn't come back to cause trouble."

"There's always trouble where you are!" she retorted angrily. She looked at her mother, her head tilted defiantly. "Jim had to try, didn't he? I'm sorry he wasn't quite good enough. But I'm not sorry he tried." Stubbornness hardened her voice. "Now, if you want us to go —"

"That's foolish talk," Amanda Rawlins said tiredly. "I've been expecting you and Jim for supper." She turned to Mel. "Don't just stand there. Help her get Jim into the house."

She held out a hand as he took a deep breath. "And I'll take that gun of yours, Mel, before you get into any more trouble."

Mel lifted the heavy weapon from the holster and handed it to her. He stood looking down at the man he had beaten, still somewhat angry, breathing harshly. His mother stepped past him and collected Jim's gunbelt from the railing and went into the house.

Marilyn shrugged. "Jim won't like it. But maybe you'd better do as Mother says. I'll take care of him inside."

Mel walked down. There was a softness in the day's afterglow, and his sister's face was a pale blur. There was strength in it, and a cold and searching curiosity; he reached down and got a hand under Jim's right arm and felt the lawman's muscles tighten as he tried to pull away.

"You didn't answer me," he said to his sister. "What's bothering him? I don't even know him."

"Jim knows you," she said. "He knows all about you. He came to Sawmill City three years ago. He and Bob became good friends. We were married last year."

They were walking up the steps. Jim Butler suddenly balked. His feet stiffened, and he jerked loose and nearly fell. He ran his fingers through his tousled hair and eyed Mel narrowly.

"I'll walk!" His voice came blurred

16

through split, swelling lips. "Yo're as tough as I heard," he added bitterly. "I'll give you that much. But I won't eat with you. And I won't stay —"

"Jim!" Marilyn's voice held urgent pleading. "Mother expects us to stay."

Jim walked to the door alone. He turned his head, leaned one hand against the wall, let his head sag a moment while he sucked in a deep breath. His arm muscles trembled.

"I'd do anything for her," he said thickly, "but not this." He looked from Mel to his wife. "Yo're his sister. Bad or good, the blood's the same. But he ain't my brother! And there's a warrant on my desk in Sawmill, Marilyn. I never told you. I didn't want you to know. But it's there. And if he's still here tomorrow, I'm coming back to pick him up!"

He pushed the door open and went inside. Mel faced his sister. She said bitterly: "Why did you come back?"

He had no ready answer. Anger made his voice cold. "Why not?" He knew his voice could be heard inside the house. . . . There was stillness there, broken only by the working of the pump handle as Jim drew water into a tin basin.

"What makes you so bitter?" His voice

17

was thin now. "You were fourteen when I left. I had my fight with Pa, not with you or with Bob or — your husband. I didn't even know him."

Her voice was low, so it would not reach the others. "I guess it's because of Paw," she said. "He needed you. We all did — and you left us. And later we heard —"

"Marilyn!" Her mother's voice was impatient.

She sighed and went past him into the house.

Mel stood looking out across the darkening yard. This was the shape of home he had carried with him. Every man has a right to rebel once, he thought angrily. He had done nothing more.

He turned and went into the house, and the old habit pattern was formed again as he dropped his hat over the peg by the door and walked into the kitchen and stood by the pump to wash his hands and face.

Jim was drying his face gingerly. He stood to one side, his shoulders held stiffly, an angry, unyielding pride keeping him from accepting even his wife's attempts at help.

He looked at Mel, his long face battered and unreconcilable. He turned to the older woman standing at the head of the round table, and his voice was low.

"I'm sorry, Ma. We won't be staying now. Tomorrow, perhaps —"

Amanda Rawlins only nodded.

It didn't seem right. Mel said roughly: "I didn't want it this way, Jim. I didn't even know you were my brother-in-law. If there is something I can say —"

"Bob said it all a year ago," Jim said. "I'll leave you be tonight, because of Ma. But tomorrow you'd best be gone. Because I'll be back — with that warrant."

Chapter II

Marilyn Butler kissed her mother briefly on the cheek and followed her husband out. There was the sound of horses wheeling, breaking into a run, fading . . . Mel stood by the sink, feeling the stiffness of his bruised face, the slow recession of his anger.

His mother said: "Supper's getting cold, Mel. We're waiting."

He washed then, and everything suddenly seemed familiar. But, turning, he missed his father's face at the head of the table, and those of his brothers. Bob, youngest of the three Rawlins boys, was blond and rakishly handsome, with a full, petulant mouth and a sensitive nature. There was a stretch of six years between Mel and Bob, but only one year separated him from Hump.

He started for the table, and suddenly stopped, feeling the blood come up and darken his face. His brother's wife, Ruth, looked at him, searching his face with grave, questioning eyes. In all this time he had not been aware she was here; yet he should have known. Ruth had lived on Stirrup since Hump had brought her home.

He stood awkwardly by his chair, and she said: "It's been a rough homecoming, Mel. Sit down. Let me be the first to say it's nice to see you again."

Amanda Rawlins' voice was stiff. "I'm sorry Jim took it upon himself to mix in family affairs, Mel. But, I, too, am glad you've come home."

And looking at her, Mel saw tears way back in her eyes, and he walked over to her and kissed her. She felt small and fragile, this woman who had borne him, and an ache came and raised a lump in his throat.

"I had to go, I reckon," he said. "I'm sorry I won't have a chance to tell Pa I'm sorry."

"It wasn't all your fault," his mother said. "Part of it was." She pulled herself together, showing a faint embarrassment under the watching eyes of her daughter-in-law. Ruth had lived at Stirrup since Hump had married her, five years ago. But she would always remain a cool and distant stranger here.

21

"Sit down and eat, son," his mother said. "You must be tired and hungry."

He didn't take his father's place at the head of the table. He sat across from Ruth and ate quietly, not saying much. Somehow, for Mel, the presence of his father and brothers was a tangible thing. They crowded the room with laughter and the rough voices of long ago.

Ruth kept searching his face. "You didn't write, Mel. We all missed hearing from you."

He didn't look at her. She was still the best-looking woman he had ever seen; the years married to Hump had made no changes he could see.

She was Doctor Elvin Sloane's daughter, better educated than most girls in that part of the country, and some people had wondered what she had seen in Hump Rawlins. . . .

"I've kept moving," he said.

"Hump wrote to you, didn't he?" Ruth's voice asked more than the question.

He looked at her now. "I got his letter last week."

Amanda Rawlins pushed her plate away. "He's gone, Mel. I don't think I'll ever get over it. Your father, then Bob, and now Hump —"

Mel pushed away from the table. He walked to the door and looked out. The lonely land lay dark under the stars. Somewhere beyond that wild, trackless country lay the sea.

Strange, he thought — *I always wanted to see the ocean.*

When they were younger, he and Hump had talked of the coast. Hump had even bet him that he would get to the sea first. . . . He had grinningly promised to bring back a canteenful for Mel.

It had been a long time ago, and they had been kids together, and there had been no hate between them . . . no Ruth. . . .

Behind him he heard Hump's wife say: "I'll wash the dishes tonight, Mother."

But Amanda shook her head. "I've done them for thirty years —"

Ruth joined him on the deep veranda. He felt her shadow beside him. The night was kind to Stirrup; he could almost believe nothing had changed.

Ruth said softly: "It's nice — at night. Who would have dreamed that Stirrup would be reduced to this?"

He turned toward her, sensing a need for talk in her tone.

"Hump left a lot out of his few letters," he said harshly. "He didn't tell me how

23

Bob felt about me. He didn't mention Marilyn marrying. He did say that Pa was dead, that Bob had disappeared. He wrote that he was riding across the desert to a little town on the coast called Manoas; that he thought all Stirrup's troubles began there."

"That was two weeks ago," she murmured. "He told me he'd be back in ten days." Her voice turned bitter. "If he wasn't back when you came, he said to tell you he'd be waiting in Manoas."

Mel put his long glance across the yard to the far run of land between the twin buttes. He felt the strong pull of that empty starlit stretch of desert that hemmed Stirrup off from the sea.

"They hit us at night, every night, for a week. Stirrup first, then Conch on the north and Straw's Tensleep to the west." Her voice was low. "It seemed like a hundred men. When it was over we buried six men — the others drifted. We lost the barn, all the horses, practically all the cattle. Many of them were shot, wantonly slaughtered. The others disappeared into that —"

He didn't say anything. He had heard there was water in the Big Sand, but no one knew where to find it. He and Hump had known this edge of the desert as well as anybody, and they had never found anything but an old Apache trail that petered out at the lava beds twenty miles in.

Several hundred head of beef, a hundred horses, could not have survived long in the desert, unless the men who had raided and plundered Stirrup had known what he and Hump and the rest of the Sawmill country men did not know.

But why? Somehow that was a nagging and insistent question in Mel's mind.

Silence lay between them — and the shadows of the past. He heard Ruth draw in a slow breath. Then she said softly: "Stirrup's still here, Mel. It could be rebuilt."

He looked down at her. She seemed strangely unmoved by the fact that her husband was gone. . . . He heard his mother working with the dishes and felt an odd distaste creep into him.

"Maybe," he said shortly. "But I want no part of it."

She peered up into his hard, bruised face, and her voice was disturbed. "No part of Stirrup? But you came back for it, didn't you?"

"I came because of Hump," he said coldly. "Because I owed him something —

something more than an explanation."

"A man with a conscience." The hurt was in her voice now; she was bitter, because she had not wanted it to show. "What about me? What do you owe me?"

"What do I owe you?"

Her face was dim and remote, and when she answered she again displayed a cool reserve. "Only you can answer that, Mel."

It nettled him.

"I ran away from Stirrup because of you," he said flatly. "You know that. I think Pa knew, too. He cornered me in the barn, and we had some bitter words, and I left. It was better to let everyone think I left because of Pa. . . ."

"How noble!" Scorn cracked her protective shell. "You think I married Hump to spite you? Well, you were right, at first, if that pleases you. But I cared for Hump. I would have made him a good wife; better than I would have made you —"

"You didn't give me a chance to find out, did you?" His voice was rough, edged with an old hurt. "You knew how I felt. One year — that's all I asked of you, Ruth. You knew I wasn't ready to settle down. I wanted to have my look over the hill — I would have always felt a restlessness, if I hadn't gone. But you and your blasted pride! You couldn't wait —"

His voice rasped deep in his throat. "Why Hump? To get back at me? To make it unbearable for me here?"

She laughed at him now, safe within her cool shell. "It was pretty bad, wasn't it?"

He turned away from her, tramped to the far end of the veranda. She didn't follow. He put his brooding gaze on the desert. There was nobody left at Stirrup except these two women. Stirrup, which had been a man's ranch, was feminine in its stillness. He knew he had to go.

For way back in Tenejo town he had heard something that had given him a clue to what had happened here. Way back in Tenejo, the night he had backed the wrong man in a card game and barely gotten away with a whole skin.

He had ridden with a rough assortment of men since he had left Stirrup. Some of them had been frankly bad. Ben Stoll was the toughest man he had come to know — and Ben had told him about Manoas. . . .

He built himself a smoke and waited, watching the rising moon. His mother came out and stood silent, drying her hands in her apron. After a while she said achingly: "They're all gone, Mel — your father and Bob and Hump. Pa's buried on the hill — Bob found him on the edge of the lava beds, with a bullet in his back. And Bob and Hump are gone, in that seaport town they call Manoas."

"I'll see what happened to them," he promised.

"No." Her voice sounded tired in the darkness. "Whatever those killers were after, let them have it. You're all I have left. I can't let you go, Mel."

"I'm tougher than Bob — or Hump," he told her. "I'm more like Pa. If Hump's still alive, I'll find him."

She sighed. "It's been like a bad dream. Only six months ago we were all here, Pa and Hump and Bob. We all came home from church with Marilyn and Jim. We had half the neighbors here. We butchered two beeves . . . we danced in the yard. Morley brought his accordion and Tony his fiddle. Now they're all gone —"

There was nothing to say. He remained on the veranda after she went in. *A man can come home to nothing.* The wind sharpened off the desert, and he heard a door close and a window open in Hump's old room and knew Ruth was going to bed.

He thought soberly, *Where was the right and the wrong? He had loved this woman who had married his brother, but he had*

wanted to be fair with her. He was a rest-
less man, not like Hump who had lost his
boyhood dreams when he grew up and no
longer cared if he never rode farther than
Stirrup's boundaries.

And Ruth had only done what she had to do. She'd been a proud girl, too proud to wait. He wanted to be fair to her tonight. His father had known, though, and his words had been brutally direct.

"There's no place for you here, son! Not with her around! Better you should leave now, before you and Hump kill each other!"

Five years of knocking around the edge of a growing country shapes a man. He thought, *I owe Hump something better than that. Hump's my brother!*

Bob and he had never been close. And Marilyn had been just a kid sister. He thought of Jim Butler, and he knew the lawman had meant what he said.

He had caused enough trouble by coming back here.

He left Stirrup in the early morning, before Ruth was up, before his mother awakened. The light was gray over the desert. He took some left-overs from the kitchen, a swig of last night's coffee, and headed across the creek, past the sagging fence toward the old Apache trail he and Hump had explored in the days when they were young and life had been simpler. . . .

Chapter III

Three days later Mel Rawlins came out of the desert to the rocky coast, and the sound of the waves against the rocks was an abrupt surprise that lifted his weary shoulders and brought an expectant look into his eyes. The breeze was suddenly cool against his hot face, and there was a hint of spray in it. And the booming of the surf was hauntingly familiar, though he had never seen the sea in his life.

He reined in on the edge of a small cove where a tiny crescent of beach glared in the lowering sun. Beyond it the sea stretched endlessly before his squinting gaze, and sunlight speckled the water with a thousand broken shafts of light.

He had found no trail through Big Sand. He had stumbled his way through, keeping southeast, riding nights, holing up during the heat of the day. He had come across an abandoned mining camp last night and followed the drifted-over ruts to this point. Now his gaze followed the newer wagon road which came in from the west and which dipped out of sight over a low ridge. Turning, he leaned on his forearms and studied the cove, his dark face expressionless.

The waves sucked and slid over weed-slick rocks, and small rollers boomed on the beach. To his right a curving headland, rising to a rocky promontory, hid what lay beyond from his casual glance. To his left the sea battered against the limestone cliffs, patiently shaping the myriad grottoes that honeycombed the steep shoreline.

He sat awhile, letting his eyes rest on the emptiness of the sea. Behind him the desert ran without a break for nearly eighty miles. . . . Stirrup seemed far away and inaccessible.

He could see no possible connection between this and the violent storm that had smashed Stirrup . . . yet his younger brother Bob had come here, and then Hump. . . .

He made a small gesture with his shoulders, pushing the memory from him. The blazing desert sun had darkened his face still more, and a three day beard roughened it. He sat loose in saddle, his gun riding low and thonged down, and there was a hard, hands-off look about him.

A tern came in from the sea, riding a

thermal current, and swooped low, asking a harsh, plaintive question of this intruder.

Mel raised a hand in mock salute.

"That's what the other fellow did, too," the girl said.

Mel brought his hands down slowly, his face stiff, like a little boy caught smoking corn fixings behind the barn. His gaze moved slowly across the cove and picked up the girl standing on a spray-whipped rock fifty feet below him.

He could have sworn she had not been there when he had first pulled up on the bluff for a breather.

She wore a man's pair of pants rolled up to her knees, and her bare legs were brown from constant exposure to the sun. A blue chambray shirt, tails free, was unbuttoned at her neck. A wide-brimmed straw hat perched precariously over chestnut hair gathered carelessly in one big mass and knotted with a piece of blue ribbon. She was holding a bamboo fishing rod from which dangled a good-sized fish.

She looked young and innocent and carefree, and for a brief moment the contrast between this girl and his brother's wife impressed itself on him and gave him an inkling how much Ruth was still in his thoughts.

"Did what?" His voice was harsh from disuse.

The girl moved up on the rock while the sea sucked and swirled around her bare feet. She wasn't afraid of him. There was frank laughter in her eyes.

"Raised his hand like that," she answered.

Idly he reached in his pocket for the makings while he debated asking this girl about Hump.

"You're smaller than the other one," she informed him, "and not so good-looking."

He grinned humorlessly. He could feel the harsh stubble on his jaw and the grit in it. He stood at six feet even, while Hump was over six feet two and weighed two-twenty, and in spite of the rounded shoulders that had given him his nickname looked big.

"What do you do besides speak to strange men?" he asked curtly.

"Fish." She held up her catch. "Seven pounds if it's an ounce," she boasted.

"Looks too big for you. You live around here?"

She pointed to the headland on his right. "Manoas."

"Come on up," he invited her. "I'll ride you into town."

She shook her head. "Dad wouldn't like it."

He shrugged. He stepped back and swung up into saddle, and when he looked down again she was gone. He straightened tall in his stirrups, puzzled, and searched the empty cove. But all he could see were the waves breaking white and lacy over the rocks. He shook his head and jogged up the wagon to the bluff.

Manoas was a coast town gone to seed. A cluster of fishing shacks huddled in an arc around a small beach and straggled up to the bluffs. The old stacks of a hide and tallow factory hung slightly back from it all, in a forlorn and abandoned gesture.

Mel followed the wagon road as it dipped down to the shore and went past a rock jetty which extended out into blue water. The first shacks crowded the beach here, just above high water. A half-dozen small fishing craft lay at anchor in the cove. Children played among the smaller boats drawn up on the sand.

Mel turned up the steep grade that led to the newer section of Manoas. A big barn sat on the bend of the road, and a sign over the big doors read: STABLES — SMITH BROS., PROPS.

A wizened-faced man dozing on a bench in the sun looked up as Mel dismounted. He had a long, sinewy neck, cross-hatched and dirty, a stump for a left arm, and an evil-smelling corncob pipe clenched between yellow stubs of teeth.

Mel leaned casually over his saddle. "Where're the others?" he asked gravely.

The one-armed man frowned. "Which others?"

"The Smiths." Mel pointed to the sign.

"I'm all there is, wise guy!" the stableman snapped. "Manassas Smith." His eyes narrowed. "Lookin' fer somethin'?"

Mel told him.

"The Sea Horse, just up the road. Drinks an' eats." He took the pipe out of his mouth and spat into the dust and lifted his eyes for a closer look at Mel.

"Puncher?"

Mel shrugged. "Off and on," he admitted.

Smith grunted. "Not many of you cow rasslers come down this far any more," he observed. "Useta be a time, though, when the taller works was goin' full blast —"

"Ever get a ship in here?" Mel interrupted. "I want to get down to Tampico."

The stableman shook his head. "Not any more." He studied Mel's hard face. . . . He was thinking that this tough-looking stranger could be on the run from the law, and that a boat to Tampico was a fast way out of the country. He remembered the others, too, and he grinned sourly.

"Yo're the third hombre in a month who's asked."

Mel's glance lay steady on the garrulous oldster. "Did they get a ship?"

"I don't know about the blond, good-lookin' kid who came first," Smith muttered. "But the big one never got out of town. One of the Mexican fishermen found his body in the cove. He's buried up on the hill there, in the mission graveyard."

Mel followed the other's pointing finger and held his stony gaze on the walls of the old Spanish mission standing aloof from the town on the high backbone of the ridge. After a moment he said: "Tough break for him." He turned and walked away, leaving the chestnut for Smith to take care of.

The Sea Horse was a square-rigged, two-story frame building dominating the shacks of lower Manoas. Mel hesitated under the creaking board sign. There was an off-sea breeze, and the smell of the sea was strong here, washing up from the kelp and the nets drying in the sun.

He spun himself a cigarette and lighted it, and then, without volition, he turned to look again at the mission. When he finally shifted his gaze his attention was caught by a coastal sailing vessel that was tacking around the high promontory into the cove.

He watched it until it dropped anchor a hundred yards from the jetty. It was a trim ship, graceful under the open blue sky, and Mel felt a stirring of admiration for it and understood why Hump had always been intrigued by the sea.

The tail of his eye caught movement on the road curling down from the ridge from which he had come and, putting his gaze on it, he saw the girl trudging down the slope. She held her pole like a rifle over her right shoulder, her pants still rolled up to her knees. He watched her swing lithely along, and he smiled as he turned and stepped inside the Sea Horse.

The big room held within it the pungent smell of salt water. A long-handled harpoon, a whaler's tool, foreign to Mel's experience, lay on pegs in the wall behind the short bar. It was the sole nautical touch in a room consisting of tables and chairs of nondescript make, and a small box piano standing incongruously in a corner.

A tall, spare-fleshed man with a shock of white hair and a black patch over his left eye was behind the bar, stropping a straight razor on a leather belt. He turned and glanced at Mel; his face was covered with freshly applied lather.

"Go right ahead," Mel said, leaning an elbow on the bar. "I can wait."

The tall man put his razor down on the counter and wiped his face on the towel. "Just shaving to kill time," he informed Mel. "What's your pleasure?"

Mel eyed the bottles lined up on the back shelf. "Old Remington will do fine."

"Good whiskey," the tall man said. He had a deep, well modulated voice Mel felt had been trained to do his bidding. Yet he did not speak like an educated man.

He set up a glass and poured, leaving the bottle on the counter. "Don't get your kind down here any more," he said conversationally. "Not since the old B and B outfit quit shipping hides."

"My kind?"

The tall man hesitated. "You smell of cows to me, stranger. But perhaps it's because I'm too close to the sea."

"I've worked with cows," Mel admitted. "Kind of drifted away from it." He dropped his gaze to his hard knuckles curled around the shot glass. "Why, it's empty," he marveled, and slid the glass to the bartender.

The tall man smiled. "So it is," he said, and refilled Mel's glass. "Every man to his own game, mister. Mine was whaling. Last ship I signed on was the Lucy Mae out of New Bedford, Massachusetts. Got paid off in San Diego and got this far back across country. Been here ever since. Fifteen years."

Mel nodded absently. "A man doesn't always wind up where he's headed."

He turned and watched the girl come into the room, carrying her pole over her shoulder. The seven-pound red snapper dangled from a short length of twine in her left hand. She looked brown and boyish in man's clothing, but viewing her close up, he saw she was older than she had first looked to him.

"Hi." Her greeting was frank and friendly.

He nodded acknowledgment as she walked by, her smile flashing at the man behind the bar. "Quit fishing when I caught this one, Tobey. I'll have it pan-fried and on the table before you wash up."

Tobias Hawkins nodded. He watched her disappear through a doorway under the open balcony that looked down on the big empty room. Then he wheeled sharply to look at Mel.

"You two met?"

There was a coldness in his voice that brought a frown to the younger man's face. He made a casual gesture. "Came out of the desert to find her fishing on the rocks east of here. I wanted to give her a lift into town, but she told me she'd rather walk."

Tobey relaxed. "You're welcome to sit in for supper, stranger. Ain't a better cook in Manoas, even if I say so myself."

"I believe you," Mel answered, smiling. "You sure," he added, "your daughter won't mind? She wasn't exactly friendly when we met."

The bar owner shrugged. "My fault, probably. There's a rough bunch of riders come through here. Most of them hang out in the Oasis, on the ridge." He pushed the bottle toward Mel, but the younger man shook his head.

"Besides, she ain't my daughter," the ex-whaler said. "And you might as well call me Tobey. Everyone else does."

"I answer to Mel," Rawlins said. He was thinking of what Manassas Smith had said, and of the grave in the mission cemetery.

41

There was a void in him he couldn't get used to. He thought of his mother, waiting on Stirrup . . . standing in the shadow of the porch and staring across the sagging fence separating Stirrup from the desert. He thought of this and knew he could not ride back and tell her that Hump, too, was dead.

"Loan Stevens is the daughter of an old friend of mine," Tobey was saying. He glanced at the harpoon, as if associating it with his friend. "When he died I promised I'd look up his family. I didn't get back to port until almost two years later. Loan's mother had died the same week. They had no near kin. Loan was five years old."

He paused as the batwings creaked. Mel turned on his elbow and watched a wrinkled Mexican woman, somber in a black rebozo, shuffle to the bar. Tobey reached under the counter for a bottle of mescal, and she put out a clawed hand. Two copper coins clinked on the counter.

Tobey shoved them back to her. "Manuel can pay me when he gets back on his feet," he said.

The woman nodded. She turned without looking at Mel, clutching the bottle to her. She shuffled out.

Mel wandered over to the piano. He ran

his fingers over the keys, tapped a high note a few times, glanced back at the saloon man.

Tobey made a gesture. "Loan plays — when she's in the mood. Sometimes she'll play all afternoon. Other times she won't go near it for a week."

Mel sat on the small stool. "Been a long time since I handled one of these things," he muttered. His mother had brought a piano with her from Virginia, and he had been the only one of the Rawlins children to show any interest in it. He ran his fingers lightly over the keys, feeling awkward and cold and remembering that the last time he had touched a piano had been at his brother Hump's wedding.

Tobey leaned on his elbows, listening to Mel break into Mendelssohn's *Wedding March*. He looked old and tired, and the easiness was gone out of his eyes.

"Say! Who's getting hitched?" boomed a new voice. The words preceded the man's hands as he parted the batwings and came into the bar.

He was a burly figure, a head shorter than Mel, with a square, weather-beaten face and a walk that had the roll and the pitch of the sea in it. He stamped in, his left hand thrust inside the pocket of his seaman's short coat, and stopped before he reached the bar, turning to stare at Mel.

"Thought it was Loan," he growled. "Didn't expect nobody wearing pants would be playing that thing."

Mel gave him a short glance and went on playing.

Tobey greeted him without much warmth. "Hello, Captain. Didn't expect you in Manoas until spring."

Captain Bremem walked to the bar, shoved Mel's glass aside and waited, scowling, until Tobey placed a clean glass in front of him. He poured his own drink out of the Remington bottle and drank it, slugging it down clean. A scowl pulled the thin white lines of an old jagged bottle scar over his right eye into an almost invisible V.

"Came up the coast from Tampico," he said surlily. "Dropped anchor to see you and Loan." He tilted the bottle again and slopped whiskey over the bar.

Mel's playing seemed to get on his nerves. Swearing, he slammed the bottle down and whirled to face Rawlins.

"Hey, you!" he rasped angrily. "Get the devil away from that piano!"

Mel glanced over his shoulder. "Speaking to me?"

"Aye," the captain snapped. He had a

reddish beard and a temper that went with it, and right now his blue eyes had a mean glint in them. "I brought that piano here for Loan, not for every tinker's son that drifts in here!"

A pulse of anger beat in Mel and brought a sharp and wicked sense of expectancy. He understood the reason for it. Normally he was a reasonable man. But Hump was dead, and probably Bob, and the whole reason for Stirrup's smashup lay buried here in Manoas.

He turned on the stool and looked the burly captain over, shrugged contemptuously, and turned back to the keys. He heard the man's gust of anger, and then Bremem's shoes slapped hard on the worn floor boards.

Tobey's voice lifted angrily. "Don't be a darn fool, Captain! He's only —"

Bremem was close when Mel turned. He didn't even rise from the stool. His pivot swung him around, and he had his Colt in his right hand, held low. The captain's forward rush, plus Mel's pivot, timed perfectly, sank the muzzle deep into the seaman's stomach.

The fight went out of Captain Bremem before he got started. He seemed to curl around Mel's fist, his angry flush fading to a lemon green. His eyes rolled back in his head.

Mel shoved Bremem away as he got to his feet. He had holstered his Colt, and to the watching Tobey, it seemed as though the Hurricane's skipper folded of his own accord.

Bremem clasped both hands across his stomach and fell across a table, slid down and pulled the table down on him. He lay there, laboring to catch his breath. For the next half-hour or so Captain Bremem was going to be a very sick man.

Mel glanced at the one-eyed saloon man. Then his gaze moved to Loan Stevens. The girl had come to the kitchen door, and the apron she had tied over her pants made her look more feminine, more like a woman.

"Sorry this had to happen, Tobey," Mel apologized, "seeing as how he's a friend of yours. And thanks for the supper invitation." He looked down at the captain. "But I reckon I better leave before he gets his breath back. No sense having to kill him."

He walked to the door, turned to look back at the girl. There was a strange expression on her face, as though she were taking a closer look at him. "Nice piano," he said. "It would have been a pleasure —"

46

The girl didn't move. Tobey waited until Mel had gone; then he started for Bremem. He stopped in the middle of the room and looked back to the batwings; he seemed different in that instant, like a gaunt, scarred lobo, smelling trouble, as yet distant and unseen. . . .

Chapter IV

Mel had enchiladas and frijoles and Mexican beer in a *cantina* on the edge of the beach. From his table near the dirty window he could see the jetty. A dinghy bobbed up and down on the small swells riding into the beach. A bony-shouldered man in a black sweater and peaked cap sat cross-legged on the edge of the pier, smoking.

Mel paid his bill and walked out. He looked up the winding cliff road to the Sea Horse, but the captain did not reappear. He reached in his shirt pocket for his Bull Durham and made himself a cigarette. He knew the game he had to play had rigid rules and that one mistake could mean sudden death. He was a man walking a tight and narrow path, and he felt a cold knot of anger in his stomach.

Beyond the jetty the schooner rode the small swells, bow lifting and falling like a woman's slow breathing. He could make out the white letters against the flaky green paint: THE HURRICANE.

Mel lighted up, his eyes on the craft, knowing somehow that she figured in what had happened to Hump. After a moment he turned and started to walk along the road winding above the fishing village. He followed it west, up past the boarded-up section of Manoas — the Manoas that had boomed when the brick kilns and the tallow factory had offered employment. The shifting tide of prosperity had ebbed away from Manoas, and it had reverted to its hard core of coastal fishing town.

Upper Manoas had been a wide open town in its day. Mel saw that the Oasis was still open, with a couple of seedy-looking characters on the porch. Several other establishments showed signs of life — but the greater part of this section of town was abandoned.

Three recently hard-run horses nosed the saloon rail, the sweat still glistening on dusty hides. He hesitated only a moment, then walked on until he found the path which led to the knoll north of town where a stone monument, ten feet high, reached its finger to the sky. Someone long ago had chiseled SALVAREZ on its rocky face.

From this knoll the adobe mission, low-roofed and badly weathered, was visible. It was slowly going to ruin, but it was still in use; someone had recently repaired the belfry where a single bronze bell hung. The rest of it had an air of tired decay.

A low brown adobe wall enclosed a small graveyard. There was no gate, although the stone pillars flanking the opening still held imbedded rusting eyebolts.

Mel walked in among the old graves. The mission wall was on his left, masses of red bougainvillea climbing and smothering the covered gallery along the cracked adobe wall. The sun slanted in over the western wall, and insects made a peaceful humming. He was in a world removed in time and space — where time and space no longer mattered.

He found his brother's grave at the southwest corner . . . a new mound marked by a wooden cross. It had one word knife-carved in the wood: HUMP. Just that — no more. Someone had thought enough about Hump to put a small Indian vase with a dozen zinnias on his grave.

Mel stood silent, feeling the wind pluck at his coat sleeves. He and Hump had parted in anger — and now there would never be anything else between them. They had been close as kids — it didn't seem right that a woman could have done this to them.

"Hello."

He turned swiftly, but checked the instinctive motion of his right hand to his gun and reached up to touch the brim of his Stetson instead. "Hello," he answered quietly.

Loan Stevens had changed to skirt and blouse. She looked older and more serious, and he was surprised to see that she reached almost to the level of his eyes. She stood on the other side of his brother's grave and looked at him; the wind ruffled her hair.

"How's the captain?"

"Feeling well enough to walk. He's gone back to the ship."

He couldn't see the cove from where he stood, but his glance was instinctive.

Loan said: "He's a friend of Dad's. They sailed together, a long time ago." She shrugged. "He probably won't be back in Manoas until spring."

"Sorry I spoiled his visit," Mel said. But anger was still in his voice, and the girl's eyes avoided him.

"I thought you'd come up here," she said, "after hearing you play the piano."

"Why?"

She indicated the grave between them. "You knew him?"

"Maybe." His voice was cold. There was nothing in his face to show how he felt.

"He knew you."

He searched her face, wondering how much she knew about him; about what had brought him there. Hump must have thought a lot of this girl to confide in her.

He described his brother. "If that's the man who's buried here, I knew him."

She nodded. "I didn't know him too well. He used to come into the Sea Horse once in a while. He kept asking about ships —"

He interrupted her. "You said he knew me. What did he tell you?"

She looked surprised. "Only that you'd be showing up soon. He said I'd know you because you'd play the piano, play the *Wedding March*."

Mel's jaw ridged. How had Hump known? Or had his brother known him better than he knew himself?

"He told me something else. He said when you showed up I was to take you to Cauldron Point and to tell you this: *'When the fog comes in!'* "

Mel's breath sucked in. "When did he tell you this?"

"Two days before he was found — in the cove."

He was silent for a long moment. He felt the girl's questioning gaze on him, but she did not put her question into words.

"Will you show me Cauldron Point?" he asked.

"Of course." She glanced at the late afternoon sun. "We can be back before dark, if we leave right away."

"Do you have a mount?"

"Manassas'll let me have one. He has the stables just below the Sea Horse. I'll meet you there as soon as I pick up a jacket —"

"No," Mel interrupted. "Meet me up the trail, by that bald butte." He indicated the point with his eyes. "I think it'll be best if we do not leave Manoas together."

Cauldron Point was a bare, rocky ridge that extended from the desolate coppery hills into the sea. It curled like a withered giant's arm against which the green swells smashed and boiled into white froth. But within the hook of this ridge the water lay quiet, and a strip of coarse sand sloped up to rocky ground.

The wind blew freely across the ridge, and the girl drew her jacket tighter about her. Mel's gaze searched the beach. There was nothing here, and he could not understand what Hump had wanted him to find.

The girl stood beside him, silent, occupied with her thoughts. He said slowly, bitterly: "There was another man in Manoas — before Hump. A younger man, blond. Smaller than either of us —"

He looked at her and caught the passage of a dark shadow across her eyes. She nodded, "I remember. He, too, kept asking about ships." She searched his face, and there was an odd questioning look in her eyes.

"What happened to him?"

"He left Manoas. He used to frequent the Oasis. He got into trouble there one night. I heard Dad tell about it. He was badly beaten. The next day he was gone —"

"You don't know where?"

"No." There was a strained reluctance in her voice. She looked out over the sea and was quiet for a spell. When she turned to him her face had a troubled look.

"We should be riding if we expect to get back to Manoas by nightfall," she suggested.

He nodded. "Just one thing," he said shortly, as they pulled back from the edge of the point. "Was Captain Bremem in Manoas the day before Hump's body was found?"

Loan shook her head. "This is the first time Captain Bremem's been in port in six months."

Mel considered this, and the strange message Hump had left for him. He turned and looked out over the slowly heaving sea, watched the haze forming in the distance, lying like a cloud bank on the water.

"Does it fog here often?"

"Sometimes, especially this time of year. Gets thick as pea soup — can't see your hand in front of your nose." She shivered and laughed lightly. "Dad doesn't let me go out when it gets fogged in. So I lie in my bed in my room and look out toward the sea and imagine that the Ancient Mariner is out there in his ghost ship, rounding the point. And the albatross hangs around his neck — and sometimes I think it hangs around mine —"

Her voice faded, and she looked out over the water, and there was an odd yearning in her attitude. But when she turned she was smiling, and a boyish twinkle was in her eyes.

"You know about the Ancient Mariner?"

"No."

"Oh — he isn't real. It's a story in verse, by Coleridge —"

"I'm not a hand for reading," he said curtly.

Her gaze moved down from the hard slant of his jaw to the gun riding the holster on his right leg. The laughter went out of her eyes.

"No," she said slowly. "I can see that —"

He studied her. She was fresh and naïve, and it made him suspicious. He had run into his share of women since leaving Stirrup, but it was Ruth who had driven the first wedge of cynicism into him. The others he had met had concealed their true nature behind a screen of flattery or coquetry. He thought of this and wondered how this girl had remained fresh and unspoiled in this backwater coastal village. Then he remembered Tobey Hawkins and understood the old seaman better.

Yet there was something about this that didn't ring true. He knew what he looked like, and yet she had readily ridden with him to this lonely point away from Manoas. . . .

"You were taking quite a chance," he said, "out here with me. For all you know I might —"

"No," she cut in, smiling. "I know you wouldn't."

"Don't ever be too sure of anything," he said harshly. He kneed his cayuse up close and reached out for her and let his hand remain in the air while a slight shock sent a tremor through him. He looked steadily into the muzzle of the small .32 caliber pistol nestling in her hand. At this distance it could kill as effectively as the heavier charge in the Colt in his holster.

"Tobey is pretty well known in Manoas," she said. "Most folks know how he feels about me. But just in case some might forget, he taught me how to use this."

Mel pulled his hand back and clasped it over his saddle horn. "I'm convinced," he admitted, grinning. "I hope you never have to use it, Loan."

Her eyes were smiling again, and it made her look young and fresh. He wondered about her. There was a lot here for a man. Then he remembered Ruth, and he felt the old knot of desire tighten in him, and he cursed his brother's wife for the way he felt now — for the hold she still had on him.

Loan's eyes danced. "You are concerned about me, aren't you?"

"Some day," he countered, "that popgun might not be enough to stop you from getting hurt."

"Oh!" She seemed surprised. "I don't

57

ride with all strangers; only those I can trust."

"And you trusted me?"

She nodded. She had a small pug nose that crinkled when she laughed. "Tipi told me you were all right."

He settled back, studying the mischievous smile in her eyes, trying to make her out. She seemed to be able to slip from a mature woman to a gamin without warning — and then it occurred to him that this girl had been brought up here in Manoas, had probably had little contact with women and been fiercely sheltered from men. He remembered Tobey's sharp hostility when he had learned that Mel and Loan had met.

"Tipi?" he said. "You lost me. I don't know any Tipi."

"You'll meet him now," she laughed. She slipped her pistol back into her jacket pocket and brought out a funny little cloth doll with a solemn Indian face painted in red and blue and yellow. It had a sad, down-at-the-mouth look that was ludicrously pathetic.

"This is Tipi. Uncle Tobey gave it to me when I was a little girl. He said it came from an island in the South Seas, from Samoa. Tipi always knows a man who can be trusted. Look." She held the doll up. "See, Tipi's smiling."

And it was. Somehow the lines around the mouth had tilted upward. It changed entirely the appearance of that sad little Indian face. He glanced at her, frowning. "How did you do that?"

"I didn't do it," she said. She was laughing softly, and he couldn't tell if she was laughing at him or at the funny little doll.

"Tipi knows me, too," she said. "He smiles when I feel good — he is solemn when I feel blue. And sometimes, when there is no one else, he understands."

Mel looked into the clear, unlined face. A girl, not yet a woman. He said softly: "I'm glad Tipi likes me."

She drew away. "I've got to get back. Tobey'll be worried if I'm not in by dark." She whirled her mare. "I'll race you to the top of the bluff."

He didn't try to catch her. She waited on the crest for him to pull up alongside. Below them lay Manoas, still out of sight behind a shouldering slope. The sun had gone down, and the sky was pale over the western hills.

He said: "I'll ride in later. Thanks for showing me Cauldron Point."

She looked at him, trying to read something in his face. "You hated him, didn't you? You came to Manoas to kill him."

The troubled certainty in her voice stiffened him. He had felt some mystery in this girl, something hidden — but this made as little sense as the trip to Cauldron Point.

"Who?"

"The man buried in the mission cemetery. The man I knew as Hump."

"Did he tell you that?"

"Yes."

The wind made a thin whistling sound among the rocks above them. It was lonelier here than any place he had ever known. . . . There was a chill in the air that seemed to reach through him.

"Don't stay in Manoas," the girl said. Her voice was urgent now. "Ride tonight, now —"

He reached out to grab her bridle, but she pulled away. He watched her ride down the darkening trail and disappear. The sound of the sea came up to him, an ancient timeless sound. . . .

The knot in his stomach took a long time to dissolve.

Chapter V

The night reached across the desert and placed a dark hand over Manoas. The sea haze hung offshore, awaiting a favorable wind. The small boats rode the ground swell, nodding like tired old men on the oily darkness of the cove.

Smith eyed Mel as the big man rode in and dismounted. He took the chestnut's bridle, started to head for a far stall, then stopped. He looked at Mel with narrowing gaze.

"Feller came in here right after you left, lookin' for you —"

Mel was rolling a cigarette. He paused, looked at the old stableman with an impassive stare. "Didn't know I had a friend in Manoas. Was he wearing a star?"

Smith showed his gums in a lopsided grin. "Not that hombre. Real craggy jasper, that one. The kind that rides on the left hand of the law, if you ask me."

Mel frowned. He stood on the ramp,

with the darkness behind him, and the glow of the lantern inside the barn outlined him. He was suddenly aware of this, and the flesh between his shoulders became acutely sensitive. He stepped inside and away from the opening and leaned back against the stable wall.

He saw Smith's eyes narrow in understanding. There was a fierce quality to this crippled old man that hinted at rougher years. He stood with his back to the chestnut and studied Mel.

There was silence between them while Mel licked his cigarette into shape and lifted it to his mouth.

"I haven't got any friends," he said. "None in Manoas."

Smith shrugged. "Yore name Mel?"

Rawlins scraped the match and lifted the flame slowly; it was a mask for the surprise he felt.

"Yeah."

"Feller said to tell you he'd get in touch with you later."

"What did he look like?"

"Tall as you, mebbe. Built something like you. He stood out there in the dark, and I didn't get a good look at him."

Mel considered the implications of this. Outside, the night was quiet, but below him was the sea, making a sound new to Mel's ears: the pounding of the surf on a small beach.

From somewhere above an accordion played a sad Mexican ballad, and with the slight shift of wind came the unmistakable sounds of voices raised in laughter.

"Celebration?" There was a casual interest in Mel's voice.

Smith seemed to weigh his answer. "Yeah. Up at the Oasis." He showed bad teeth in a mirthless grin. "It happens every so often."

Mel picked shreds of tobacco from his lips. His eyes had a bland regard. "Might join in the fun. Been on my lonesome too long, I reckon. Man needs company once in a while, to keep human."

"Depends what kind of company," Smith snapped. He turned away, taking the chestnut with him.

Mel grinned sourly. He went out and stood on the walk and looked down at the cove. The Hurricane had upped anchor and left, and this puzzled him. It left him with a vague unrest; it added to the disquiet which nagged at him.

It seemed certain that Bob, too, was dead. He couldn't go back to Stirrup and face Ruth and his mother with this bitter fact without knowing why Bob and Hump had been killed.

He pondered what had brought Bob here before Hump. He should have asked more questions at home, found out more about what had happened at Stirrup. But his brother-in-law would not have given him time. He smiled bleakly at the thought that he was kin to a lawman.

Bob had asked about ships. And Hump had, too. And he had left a cryptic message that had to add up to something. *When the fog comes in!*

Somehow Captain Bremem and the Hurricane figured in Stirrup's trouble. . . .

He turned and walked up the hill and stopped on the narrow crooked street paved with old red bricks. The roofs of the shacks of lower Manoas lay below him, huddled like sheep, and the sea was a vast rolling mystery, reaching out to the stars that clung just above the horizon.

Behind him the tallow factory lay mute and abandoned under the eyes of the night. And off to the right, dark against the shapeless surface of the land, was a series of brick ovens, looking like igloos he had seen in picture books in school.

This, too, lay dark and silent, a victim of the economic recession that had hit

Manoas. The lights of the Oasis splashed out into the narrow street, and the rack was crowded with horses. Mel turned and walked toward the saloon, drawn by the sounds of rough celebration and a cold curiosity.

Loan Stevens lay on her stomach on her bed in the dark. She had the room which made a dormer over the street, and from her bed she could look through the window to the cove and the mystery of the night. She lay there now, listening to the sad wail of the accordion from the Oasis.

She had played her part, as she had been told. But a feeling of guilt kept her awake and restless. Her thoughts were full of the man who had ridden to Cauldron Point with her.

She tried to fit him into the pattern they had described. But the edges were rough and didn't fit smoothly.

Usually she read herself to sleep. But books were not enough tonight, nor the night's dark mystery. She turned and lay flat on her back and stared up at the dark ceiling. Old yearnings wracked her. Manoas was a backwater coastal town and she had no friends. Tobey didn't want her to associate with the Mexicans, and there was no one else. The percentage girls up in the Oasis were a hard and cynical lot who had no interest in her, and there was enough of the Puritan in her upbringing to make her shy away.

"Just another year," Tobey had told her. "Then we'll leave Manoas and go East where you'll meet a lot of people. There's a small village near Boston named Dedham. I was born there. . . ."

She turned over and buried her face in her arms. Somewhere down in the big barn of the house a door opened and closed. It crept into her awareness, rousing her with its implication of secrecy.

She sat on the edge of the bed and listened. There was something going on in Manoas, something with which Tobey was connected. She had known it for months now, and distrusted it. She had pulled back from it, not wanting to know what it was, feeling that it could only hurt her.

But curiosity prodded her now. She got up and walked to her bedroom door. Her bare feet made no noise, and for once the old floor boards did not creak. She turned the knob very slowly and opened her door a few inches.

". . . He was here." Tobey was talking. There was a sharpness to her foster father's voice such as she'd seldom heard. "He's tougher than you said. He handled Captain Bremem like a baby."

The other voice was blurred, but Loan Stevens knew who it was.

"I don't like it!" Tobey's voice rose angrily. "I want him out of the way! He's cagey. And I'm not sure we fooled him with that grave and Loan's story —"

"We'll do it my way!" the other voice broke in. It had a harsh insistence. "An old score, Tobey. You promised. Or I'll —"

They moved away, as though Tobey suddenly realized they could be overheard. They were in darkness below, for Tobey had put out all the lights in the Sea Horse except the one turned low at the stair landing.

She listened, straining to hear more. But the voices were only a murmur now. She thought of the man she had taken to Cauldron Point and remembered less what she had been told and more the easy humor in him, the way he had laughed with her at Tipi and not at her. It was hard to believe he was a killer, paid to hunt down a man in Manoas.

She went back to the bed and lay on her back and listened to the accordion. From experience she knew only Manoas, but

67

there was a wider world with which she was familiar. The world of Dickens and Thackeray and Hawthorne . . . the worn, often-read books that substituted for life. But tonight they did not comfort her. She kept thinking of a rough-bearded man with gray eyes and an easy smile, and the pain building up inside her had a tearing sweetness she did not understand. She buried her face in her pillow and wept, because all the dreams of her childhood no longer mattered and growing up was hard.

Out on the small beach the waves washed in with rhythmic beat, older than Manoas, older than the hills that looked down on them.

The Oasis was built like a barn, big and roomy, with a high-raftered ceiling, a bar that took up two walls, and stairs that led to a number of small private rooms.

The accordianist sat on the edge of a small table under the balcony. He played with his eyes closed, a small, wiry, scarred Mexican who seemed isolated in his own particular world of pain and oblivious to his surroundings.

Mel halted just inside the slatted doors to get his bearings. He picked out a big blond man pushing a hard forty, wearing a striped silk shirt and gaudy armbands, standing at the corner of the north bar. Behind him a closed door told whoever was interested that this room was PRIVATE.

Five shaggy-haired men, sheepmen who ran small flocks east of Manoas, were grouped clannishly together at the west bar. They were silent and self-consciously minding their own business.

Ranged along the north bar, standing a little apart from the blond man in the striped shirt, was another group, different from the sheepmen, more arrogant, lean, thin-lipped. They wore range clothes and all had belt guns. A tough wild crew, they were vociferous in their talk and their remarks.

Three day laborers from the small mining town of Selby were grouped somewhat conspicuously around a table near the bar. They were watching one of their number pit his strength against a squat, blocky Navajo — but they were silent in their partisanship. The riders at the north bar were making all the noise, and the miners, like the sheepmen, were keeping a tight lip.

"Get him, Bull!" one of the gunmen was urging. He was a lean, sinewy-necked man with a cast in his left eye. "Put some of

69

that suet behind it. Show that Injun a white man is worth two of his kind."

The Navajo's obsidian eyes flicked up to the heckler. Then, as though he had been playing with the heavy miner, he forced the man's hand down on the table.

Bull got up, shame-faced. He walked to the bar, avoiding the sneering remarks of the range men, and tossed a coin on the counter. "Give the Injun his drink," he told the bartender.

The Navajo settled back, his ugly dark face impassive. Mel walked past his table, headed for the bar.

The Navajo's arm stopped him. *"Señor,"* the Indian challenged, "you try strength with Chief?"

Mel looked down at him. The Navajo looked as wide as the table; a dirty shirt cloaked his heavy shoulders. His face was rust-brown, his nose flattened so that only the nostrils were raised above the hard planes of his face. He had little beard, and his eyes shone with a contemptuous glint. A chicken feather was stuck in his greasy black hair, held in place by a dirty yellow silk ribbon tied around his forehead.

He smelled bad.

"Some other time, Chief," Mel said, and started to pull away.

The Indian's fingers tightened on his arm. "All strangers play, white man."

The hardcases at the north bar had turned to look at Mel. The man who had been yelling encouragement to Bull gibed, "Yeah — you look pretty big, fella. Give the Navajo a try."

The Chief's voice was insolent. "Try um, stranger. You lose, you buy drinks. Okay?"

Mel hesitated. He could pass this up, but it occurred to him that this probably was the usual procedure whenever a big man showed up for the first time at the Oasis. The Chief put on a show for them and earned himself his drinks.

He shrugged. "I'll give it a try, Chief."

He loosened his coat and sat down, facing the Navajo across the table. Behind him he heard Bull say, "I got fifty on the Indian, Mike."

Mel grinned. He put up his hand, and the Chief's fingers closed hard around his palm, and someone in the bar line yelled: "Now!" and Mel threw a savage burst of strength into his move.

It caught the Navajo by surprise, and Mel gained an advantage in that moment. He had the Chief's arm bent toward the table, and now the leverage was with him. He saw the Navajo's face bead with sweat.

71

The muscles knotted under that torn, dirty shirt.

Rawlins' grin went tight. But he held his advantage, though the muscles seemed to crack in his shoulders. He saw the Chief's black eyes suddenly show uncertainty, and then he knew he had the man.

Someone muttered, "Cripes! The Navajo can't budge him!"

He felt a quiver start in the Chief's forearm, and he put everything he had behind his downward thrust. The Navajo's arm suddenly collapsed. His knuckles cracked against the table top, and his breath gusted out.

Mel got up. The Indian's eyes held a sullen respect.

"Thataboy, fella." The sinewy gunman's voice attracted Mel's attention. "Always figgered that Injun was a false alarm."

The Chief looked at him. "You likeum try, False Eye?"

The man's smile slid from his face. His companions grinned. "Go ahead, Turk. Give the Chief a whirl."

"I'll give him a slug between his teeth!" Turk snarled.

The Chief grunted and settled back. Mel stepped up to the bar.

"Yo're buyin' this round, Turk," the man

next to Mel said. "Include the stranger, too." He was older than the others, weatherbeaten, his white hair startling against his mahogany-hued features.

Turk scowled at Mel. "What're you drinkin'?"

"Same as the rest of you," Mel said. He watched the bartender pour. The others were eyeing him, and up close he saw they were a hard lot. He picked up his glass, and the white-haired man said: "Let's drink to him, boys. First man ever came to Manoas who put the Chief's arm down."

The others drank. Mel said, "I wouldn't want to try him again."

The other grinned. "You got him fair, fella." He slid his glass back for a refill and looked at Mel. "I'm Tane," he said.

His eyes were on Rawlins, smiling, but way down deep there was a cold and deadly menace. Rawlins met his look. "I answer to Mel." He let it stand at that.

As he said it, he wondered which one of these men knew him. He had recognized no one here, but someone had asked for him at the livery — someone in Manoas knew him.

Tane's voice held only a casual interest. "Staying in town a spell?"

"Maybe." Mel glanced at his drink.

"Friend of mine recommended Manoas. Said it was a quiet place, and a man could stay out of trouble."

"I wouldn't know," Tane answered. His voice held no inflection. "Me and the boys don't get down here very often. We ride for the Big T spread, north of here."

You're a liar! Mel thought. But he kept this to himself. He knew there was no cattle ranch and little else between Manoas and the north this side of Stirrup.

"Might be you're the gent I was told to see," he murmured. "Friend of mine said if I ever got down this way to ask someone in the Oasis about *El Patrone* —"

Tane put his glass down in a slow and deliberate manner. The man next to him had caught Mel's words; he stood quiet, a crooked smile on his lips.

Tane wasn't smiling. He said: "That friend of yores — he got a name?"

Mel shrugged. "I told him I'd forget, unless the boss asked. You him?"

Tane began to chuckle. "Might be. But I reckon you better talk to Carl there. That's him — just going into his office."

Mel looked. "Doesn't strike me like the gent my friend told me about."

"Mebbe he ain't," Tane said. His voice was blunt. "But I reckon you might ask."

74

"I'll do that," Mel nodded. He took out a ten-dollar gold piece and pushed it toward the bartender. "I'm buying the next round. And squeeze a drink out of this for the Chief."

Carl Spencer was behind his desk when Mel closed the office door behind him. He stood and waited while Carl's ice-blue eyes looked him over.

"Got something on your mind, stranger?"

"I'm looking for *El Patrone,*" Mel said

Carl rolled his cigar from one corner of his mouth to the other. "What's the joke?" His voice was cool, skeptical. "Some of the boys send you in here?"

Mel frowned. Had Ben Stoll been kidding him? It didn't seem likely; Ben had little humor in him. And he had been serious that night. Ben could not have known about Stirrup, for Mel had never talked about it. The tipoff about Manoas, and whom to see, had been just that — it had been Ben's way of saying thanks for the help Mel had given him.

"If it's a joke, it's on me," Mel admitted.

Carl studied him. His gaze seemed to grow remote, pull back in on itself. After a while he said: "You looking for a job?"

"If it's a long way from the law," Mel replied. "I'm more interested in getting down to Tampico."

"That's a hole," Carl said. "No place for a good man."

"I'm not choosy!" Mel snapped. His anger was rising, and he kicked it along. "Forget it. I guess my friend played a joke on me, at that. But if I ever run across the son again, it'll be my turn to laugh!"

He started to turn toward the door, and Carl said: "Proddy, eh?" He was grinning faintly. "Stronger than you look, too. I saw you put the Chief's arm down. Ain't never seen anyone do it — and some pretty powerful boys have tried."

"Muscle isn't what I trade on," Mel said flatly.

Carl nodded. "Pretty good with that Colt?"

"Better than most," Mel replied coolly.

Carl grinned now. "You sound tough and you look tough. What's your name?"

"Mel."

"Mel what?"

"It could be Smith, or Jones, or anything else. But Mel's enough for my friends."

Carl shrugged. "Touchy, too." He leaned back; then his voice picked up as Mel wheeled for the door. "Whoa, Mel. Just a minute! Maybe we can use you."

Mel looked back. "We?"

"Yeah. I don't have the say. But come back tomorrow night. I'll let you know."

Mel hesitated. The anger went out of him slowly. "I'll be back," he promised, and went out.

Chapter VI

Mel walked back to lower Manoas. The salt tang of the sea gave him a strange exhilaration. He stopped by the Sea Horse, but the windows were dark and he decided against getting Tobey up.

He went on down to Manassas Smith's stables. Smith was apparently asleep. Mel stood in the yard and wondered where he could spend the night. There didn't seem to be a place in Manoas that could put up a traveler.

He rolled a cigarette and brought the match flame to his face; the voice from the dark held a querulous urgency. "Put that blamed thing out!"

He puffed the flame out almost instantaneously with the order. Smith's reedy voice held a vast disgust. "Thought you had better sense!"

"Thought you were asleep," Mel snapped. He was nettled. He searched the darkness of the stable yard but made out no one.

"I sleep light," Smith said. He moved and became a thicker blob against the darkness. "What you looking for? Figgerin' to sneak out without payin' yore bill?"

"I'm looking for a place to bunk out!" Mel snarled.

"Didn't the boys up at the Oasis take to you?" Mel detected a thin sarcasm in the old man's tone.

"I didn't ask." Mel felt silly; the cigarette still dangled from a corner of his mouth. Defiance shoved caution aside; he scraped another match and said, "To blazes with you, Smith!" and lighted his cigarette.

Smith faded back and became a voice again. "No fool like a stubborn young one!" he muttered. "You want a place to sleep?"

"That's the general idea."

"You might try the beach —"

"Sounds like the smartest advice I've had tonight," Mel said coldly. He started to turn away, temper riding his stiff shoulders.

"Aw, don't be so danged muley," Smith called. "There's clean hay up in the loft, and if you'll open the winder you'll get the smell of the outgoing tide instead of manure."

Mel hesitated. He was beginning to feel

the effects of the trip across the desert, the dismal events of the day. He turned back.

"Get rid of that butt," Smith said. "And," he added quietly, "rest quiet. I sleep light — an' disturb easy."

Mel sensed the underlying friendliness in the old man's voice; he wondered at the reason for it. He shrugged. "Thanks, Smith." And dropping his cigarette butt, he stepped on it before going into the barn.

Mel rolled over and felt the sun in his eyes, awakening him. He lay for a while soaking in the strange sound of the pounding surf on the beach, trying to identify the tidewater smells.

Hay tickled the back of his neck, and he sat up. Through the small window opening he could see the early sunlight on the sea. It made a track into the far distance, like a line of copper drawn to infinity.

He was hungry. He rolled over and found the rickety ladder and came down into the barn and started beating the hay out of his clothes with his hat. He checked the working of his gun, an ingrained habit, then jammed his hat on his head and ran his fingers across the stiff bristle on his jaw.

Smith was nowhere in sight. Mel poked

his head into the tiny cubicle where Smith slept, but the old man was not in. Leaving the stable yard, Mel walked down to the Mexican section of Manoas, stopped in at the café for breakfast, and asked the whereabouts of a barber.

The man behind the counter shook his head, spread his hands, bared his teeth in an uncertain grin. If he understood English he gave no indication of it. But Mel got the general idea. He paid for his meal and went back to the stables.

Smith was on the bench, in the same position as when Mel had first seen him. He looked at Mel as though they had not seen each other the night before.

"I need a shave," Mel said.

"Got a razor?"

Mel nodded. "Brush, too. Plumb out of soap, though."

"Use mine. Water in the barrel behind the barn —"

Mel shaved in Smith's room. There was a mirror on the shelf by the window, and he did a creditable job. Smith walked in just as he cut himself once, under the left ear.

"You had a visitor last night," Smith said, quiet-voiced. He blocked the doorway.

Mel turned. "I didn't hear anyone —"

"He didn't come into the yard. Stayed out on the walk. He was just a shadow — but he stayed a long time." Smith grinned. "I was ready for him, if he'd come in —"

Mel rinsed his face, dried himself. "Right shy hombre," he observed dryly. He walked outside and into the barn and saddled up. Smith watched him ride out of the yard, narrow speculation in his old eyes.

Mel rode out of town and over the first ridge toward Cauldron Point. The sun lifted above the offshore haze and warmed the land. The offshore breeze was damp against his face.

He rode to the edge of the bluffs which formed Cauldron Point and studied the sea. The tide was in and the water swirled deep below him. . . . He looked out over the restless water, wondering what connection there could be here with what had happened to Stirrup.

He rode back and down into the small protected beach and then inland for a bit. He ran across a short stretch of wagon tracks, old and drifted over, and these faded out on hard malpais. The tracks had no visible beginning and ending . . . they were there, like an odd piece of the puzzle he was trying to put together.

He rode back to the beach and ground-reined the chestnut among the high rocks. The cove was small and protected and lonely; the gulls wheeled and made raucous cries in the sky.

He had never splashed around in anything deeper than the South Fork of the Salt, and the waves breaking on the sandy beach fascinated him. He undressed, placed his gunbelt carefully on top of his clothes, and went into the sea.

The waves broke against his chest and knocked him back, and he gasped at the impact. He had learned to swim, but this was different. He ducked into the next breaker, and it tumbled him around. He got salt water in his mouth and gagged; he stood up and floundered shoreward, coughing.

The shot made a flat, ugly sound in the otherwise quiet cove!

He froze. He was close enough to shore so that the waves broke and frothed against his thighs. He brushed water from his smarting eyes and studied the man who had fired the shot.

The rifleman was hunkered down beside Mel's clothes, the rifle across his knees. He had Mel's Colt thrust in his waistband and was reaching in his vest pocket for a ready-made cigarette. He lighted the smoke with the same hand — his right hand never left his rifle.

Mel grinned as he recognized the man. His feet made prints on the wet sand as he came ashore.

The other chuckled coldly. "Scared the stuffing out of you, didn't I?"

Mel shrugged. Water dripped from his hair into his eyes. He shoved a hand through it, shoving hair back from his face.

"Glad it was you, Ben." His voice held a quick welcome.

"It could have been somebody else," Ben Stoll said. The smile on his lips held no humor. He was as tall as Mel, but narrower through the shoulders, thinner in the flanks; a gaunt, gray lobo of a man who walked warily, made little noise, but killed quickly when he had to. Mel had a grim respect for the guns this man packed.

Mel nodded. "Could have," he agreed.

"You'd be floating out there now, if it had been," Ben said. He got up, moved into the shadow of the higher rocks. And he didn't put down his rifle.

"Get dressed," he said. "You look like a darn fool standing there."

Mel grinned. He got into his clothes, tugging his socks over his wet feet. It must have been Ben who had asked for him last night, he thought. He felt better, knowing that Ben was here. Once he told Ben what the trouble was —

He turned and looked into the deadly muzzle of Ben's rifle!

He didn't get it right off. He stared at the gun, at the change in Ben's face. There was no welcome in it, no hint of former friendship.

"The fun's over, kid." Ben was not more than six or seven years older than Mel, but he had always called him "kid."

"I didn't know it had started," Mel said. There was no mistaking the hostility in Ben's face, the bleakness in his eyes. "We parted friends once. You even told me whom to contact if I ever got down this way and wanted a job —"

"You tell Carl Spencer who sent you?"

"No."

Ben's face didn't change, but his eyes held a murky relief. "Kid," he said slowly, "I'm gonna speak my piece just once. I was sent to kill you. But I owe you something for that night in Tenejo. Get on that cayuse and clear out of here. Don't come back to Manoas!"

Mel's jaw ridged. "No. I'm looking for a job, and Carl Spencer said to come back —"

"Carl didn't know," Ben said. "But he knows now. You step inside the Oasis, and you're a dead man, kid!"

Mel's lips pulled back against his teeth. "Why, Ben?"

"I can't tell you. But if you stay, I'll get you. That's plain, kid. I'll get you!"

He stepped back slowly, and tossed Mel's gun into the sand. "For old times' sake, kid — get out of here!"

Mel waited, listening to the swirl and roll of the waves around the rocks. Then he saw Ben, mounted on a big sorrel horse, top the ridge, move along it for a spell, and dip down out of sight. Ben didn't look back once.

Mel knew that Ben Stoll had meant what he had said. He walked up to his gun and blew sand from it, fighting the empty, sick feeling in his stomach.

Chapter VII

The sunlight thinned, and the day seemed to lack warmth as Mel rode back to Manoas. A layer of high, fleecy clouds pushed across the sky from the Gulf, and the wind freshened and felt damp against his cheeks.

Mel rode back slowly, a stubborn light in his eyes. He didn't want trouble with Ben, and he'd try to avoid it. But he had come to Manoas because his brother had sent for him. Hump was dead. Now he had to find out who had killed him — and who was behind Stirrup's smashup.

Somewhere here, along this desolate coast, lay the answer. And Ben Stoll was part of it!

He came down into the small cove and stopped to watch a cluster of Mexicans on the beach. Two fishing boats were heading out, hoisting small, patched sails while the group watched. The mission priest was there, holding a big wooden cross, and the gathering knelt on the sand and prayed for the safe return of the fishermen.

Mel shifted in saddle, lifting his gaze to the town above the cove. There seemed to be little connection between Upper Manoas and those who lived along the beach, and he had the feeling there were two ways of life here: one old and tied to the sea; the other raw and violent and as impermanent as the desert winds.

His jaw had a tight, grim slant as he eyed the town. Ben Stoll had meant what he had said. Mel knew he'd have to face Ben if he stayed, and he didn't fool himself — he knew it meant taking the biggest gamble of his life. And even killing Ben would not make things different. Someone in Manoas knew who he was; knew what he was after. Even Ben had not known. But the fact that someone had recognized him meant that his talk with Carl Spencer was off now. *El Patrone,* whoever he was, was not going to give him another chance.

The choice before him was like a mailed fist held under his nose. He could take Ben's advice and leave Manoas. After all, Hump was dead. And he had the depressing feeling that Bob Rawlins was dead, too. Getting himself killed now wouldn't help what was left of Stirrup. It wouldn't make things easier for his mother.

The decision was his to make, and he waited, not quite certain what was the best course to follow. Up on the hill across the cove, the golden cross of the old mission caught the sun, and he had the thought that it had been built there purposely, as a marker for the Spanish galleons which had sailed across this stormy Gulf from the distant shores of Mexico and even from Spain.

Mel Rawlins' face was bleak as he checked his guns.

He rode up the narrow, winding road and dismounted in front of the Sea Horse. He could hear Loan Stevens singing inside, and again he was struck by the young, clear innocence of this girl. It arrested him for a moment; then he smiled and went inside.

Loan was sweeping out the place. She had a yellow silk scarf knotted over her hair, and the sleeves of her blouse were rolled to her elbows, and her faded blue Levi's were rolled to her knees. She looked gaily efficient, and when he came in she had just pulled a chair away from a table and was sweeping under it.

She stopped sweeping and stood up

straight; her smile of greeting was brief and uncertain.

The place was empty. Mel half expected to see Tobey step through the curtained doorway behind the bar. But Loan's foster father was not in sight.

He came into the room, and Loan said in a small, still voice: "I thought you had gone."

He shook his head. "I'll be leaving right after dinner."

"Oh?"

"Where's Tobey?"

"He went out a few minutes ago. He's checking an order with Leo, who does our freighting."

Mel shrugged. "It wasn't important. I just wanted to say goodbye." He took out papers and tobacco and started to roll a cigarette.

She didn't say anything, and he looked away, remembering the last time he had been there. "I'm sorry about the captain," he said. "He didn't stay long, did he?"

"He never does. Comes in and has a few drinks with Dad. Then we don't see him again for months."

"What's his business?"

She shrugged. "He used to be a whaler. But I don't think the Hurricane is a whaling ship. She's a trader —"

"Does he ever pick up cargo in Manoas?"

"Not that I know of," she replied. "Sometimes he brings something for Tobey — that piano, for instance. But since the brick and tallow factories went out of business, there has been no regular shipping in Manoas."

"About that young blond fellow, the one who took the beating in the Oasis," he said, changing the subject abruptly, "does Tobey know what became of him?"

She knuckled the tip of her nose thoughtfully. "Nothing more than I told you. Why? Did you know him?"

Mel nodded soberly. "He was my brother. So was Hump."

Loan Stevens sat down. She slackened into the chair, surprise stamped on her face. Her mouth remained open while she stared.

"Hump — is — your brother?"

"He was. So was Bob." Mel's voice was hard. "That's why I came to Manoas. Hump wrote me to meet him here —"

"You're lying!" She was stiff now, her face red, angry. "You're just trying to get me to tell you —" She stopped, her gaze shifting to the door.

Tobey's voice rang out harshly in the room. "What are you doing here?"

Mel turned. The Sea Horse owner had just come in. He seemed surprised to find Mel there, and displeased.

Mel said: "I came in to say goodbye. . . ."

Tobey walked to the bar, went behind it. He faced Mel over the counter, his bony face hostile. "All right. Say it and get out!"

Mel stiffened, and the back of his neck became red. "Kinda changed, ain't you, Tobey? What happened? You in with Ben?"

He saw a small gleam light up in Tobey's eye, and he knew there was a connection.

But Tobey denied it. "I don't know any man named Ben." He lifted his hands from below the counter and leveled a shotgun across the bar. "But I know your kind, fella. They come and they go. They cause trouble, and they get into trouble. I don't want your kind hanging around Loan."

"Why don't you let Loan pick her own kind?" Mel cut in harshly. "She's old enough!"

"Loan'll do what I say! Now get out of here!"

Mel took his hard gaze from the shotgun, looked at Loan. She was white-faced. He said bluntly: "Someone's been lying to you, Loan. I don't know why. But

92

what I told you is true. I came to Manoas to find out what happened to them. And —"

"Get out!"

Mel turned. Tobey had cocked the hammer of the shotgun, and there was a quiet deadliness in his manner that convinced Mel. He nodded, dry-lipped.

"Some day, girl, you'll know —"

He turned on his heel and went out and stood awhile in the sun, letting its thin warmth soak the chill from his spine. He didn't hear any sound from inside, and he felt sorry for Loan. But there was nothing more he could do here without killing Tobey or getting killed.

He mounted and rode back to the stables. Smith was cleaning out the stalls.

"Thought you'd gone," he said. His voice was noncommittal.

"Owe you for a night's lodging," Mel said. "I make a habit of paying my bills."

"I'll take a dollar for the hoss," Smith said. "The lodging's free." He pocketed the money Mel gave him. He stood a moment, leaning on the pitchfork, his old eyes studying Mel.

"They scared you out, eh?"

Mel grinned briefly. "You can call it that."

"Reckon yo're smart, at that," Smith answered. "Smarter'n the blond kid who came here first, about three months ago."

Mel said slowly: "I knew him. Wondered what happened to him."

Smith reached into his overalls for a lint-speckled piece of chewing tobacco. "If yo're really interested, you might take a ride to Tallow. Old wagon road starts back of the brick kilns. Foller it north an' you'll run smack into the old gold camp."

"Tallow?"

"Yep. Petered out four, five years ago." Smith wiped spittle from his chin. "Never amounted to much. Jasper called Reynolds named it. Reynolds worked in the tallow factory here, but liked to fool around in the hills, looking for gold, on his days off. Ran into some yeller stuff back there an' started a stampede. Nobody got rich. A few lost their shirts. But you'll find Tallow there —"

"And Bob?"

Smith shrugged, his eyes lidded.

"You knew Bob?"

"He kept his cayuse here. Didn't have the same brand as yores. Strange iron — looked like a Stirrup. Only saw one other like it, on a cayuse ridden by a bigger hombre, feller who called himself Hump."

"I knew him, too," Mel muttered. "He's dead, you said?"

"Did I?" Smith turned to his pitchfork.

Mel caught an odd note in the old man's voice, and it sent a crawling sensation through him. "Hump's buried up in the mission graveyard," he said coldly. "I saw the grave."

"Reckon he's dead, then," Smith said. He began working, ignoring Mel.

Rawlins' mouth went crooked. Smith was a tight-lipped codger. He knew he'd get nothing more from him at this time. But what he hadn't said told Mel plenty.

It opened up a possibility he had not considered. And the more he examined it, the more it began to explain some of the things that had puzzled him.

He backed the chestnut away from the stall and mounted. He leaned over the horn, his voice even. "Thanks for the tip, Smith."

The stableman leaned on his pitchfork. "I didn't say a thing. . . ."

Cigar smoke made a thin blue haze against the ceiling in Carl Spencer's private room. He had two important visitors, but he was not satisfied with either man, and an unspoken rancor lay between them, making the silence somewhat strained.

Carl stood by his window, the cigar between his teeth giving him a squat, bulldog look. He parted the lace curtains and looked down on lower Manoas and watched Mel Rawlins come out of the stable yard and head down the cove trail.

He glanced at the tall, gaunt man lounging against the wall. "You should have killed him, Ben!" His tone was accusing.

Ben shrugged. "He did me a good turn once. We're rid of him. He's leavin' town, ain't he?"

The big man sitting with his legs crossed in the stuffed wing chair gave a harsh laugh. He was smoking one of Carl's cigars, but he was no cigar smoker.

"He'll be back, Ben!"

Ben Stoll gave him a quick, bleak look.

Carl said, "I hope not. We've got enough trouble without bothering with a footloose gunslinger. The Border Patrol's got a couple of men snooping around. We've got to figure on a way to get rid of them without bringing the whole force down on Manoas. And Bremem ain't gonna wait all summer —"

"He'll be back!" The big man had a dark, brooding look.

Carl frowned. "Why do you say that? Do you know him?"

"I know him better than Ben does." His voice was thin with an old, bitter hate. "The boys should have killed him last night."

Carl nodded. "Ben," he said sharply, "better follow him. We don't want him back!"

Ben straightened. He gave a long, hard look at the man in the chair. "I'll take care of him," he said. He crossed the room with the silent prowl of some gaunt lobo, and went out.

The big man got up and joined Carl at the window. A pair of field glasses lay on Carl's dresser; he took them and peered through the pane, focusing on the rider just topping the ridge on the east side of the cove.

"He's changed some," he muttered. He shifted slowly to look out over the cove. Even under high magnification, he could barely make out the craft lying to at the edge of the horizon.

"Captain Bremem will bring her back as soon as the night fog gets thick enough," he muttered. "We'll have to take a chance on the Border Patrol —"

Carl Spencer shook his head. "The boss

said to wait. You know how he feels. He doesn't want anything to go wrong. And he wants to be sure Rawlins is out of the way before the Hurricane comes back in."

The big man handed Carl the glasses. "Think Ben will see to it?"

Carl shrugged. "Ben usually does what he's told."

"Think he's fast enough?"

Carl looked surprised. "Ben?" He began to laugh. "I wouldn't worry about Ben. Not a bit. . . ."

Chapter VIII

The abandoned brick kilns were contained within an acre of ground behind a tumble-down shed. Broken brick lay scattered between the old furnaces, some of them hidden by weeds or drifting sand. In the hills behind the kilns lay the great gouge in the red earth that had provided the clay for the bricks. The narrow gauge rails that had brought the mule-drawn carts down to the kilns lay rusted in the sun.

Mel came upon the old road from the east. Five years had all but wiped out the wagon ruts.

He gave the chestnut a breather while he surveyed the scene. The town of Manoas was just behind him, but it was hidden by the rise of the ridge, and a newcomer here would be unaware that the sea was just beyond.

The burned hills lifted to the north, ugly and sterile and stony, patched by sage and greasewood and occasional ocotillo. Here and there in the long stretch of barren coastline, narrow valleys broke through to the Gulf, and it was in these that sheep-men ran their flocks.

The wagon ruts led north toward Stirrup. But Stirrup, Mel knew, lay another sixty miles farther north, behind three desolate ranges that ran parallel to the coast.

He followed the road into the hills, and almost immediately the temperature changed. The offshore breeze was shut off here, and the hills held the heat, boxing it around him. He felt the silence press against his ears, and because of it he remembered the surf's undertone with which he had become familiar.

He paused to wipe his face, and all at once he felt uneasy. He grew instantly alert, having lived too long with violence not to heed this premonition. He made no sudden move. But when he topped a small rise he turned to look back.

He saw no one. But a slow cloud of dust lingered between the low hills through which he had just passed.

He waited a long while until the dust settled, and still no one appeared. It did not satisfy him. He turned the chestnut, but now he rode with his weight in his stirrups, and his eyes kept a constant watch around him.

He came upon Tallow suddenly!

He rounded a hill and it was there, a cluster of old, weatherbeaten shacks clinging to the sides of raw, desolate hills. Cottonwoods made a splash of pale green in a draw just south of the only two-decker building in the group.

The town seemed as dead as the hills. Yet uneasiness rode with Mel. He scanned the building line as he jogged down the single sandy street. Most of the buildings were on his left, and the bare hills rose behind them.

His horse smelled water and picked up its gait, heading for the cottonwoods. The sagging two-decker had a board sign hanging askew over the door: REYNOLDS HOUSE.

He heard nothing above the insect hum in the draw; the silence clinging to this old ghost town was hot and still. But his wariness didn't leave. He felt like a man with a hidden gun trained on his back, the muzzle following him down that forgotten street to the draw.

A small spring bubbled up and made a small pool under the cottonwoods, its overflow losing itself in the sandy earth a dozen yards beyond. Mel dismounted and let the chestnut drink, while he felt in his pockets for the makings.

And as he waited by the stallion he knew Ben was there! He couldn't explain it, but he knew! Ben was somewhere in this shabby old town, waiting for him with a cocked gun!

Mel began to sweat. Ben had warned him. And he should have known Ben well enough to realize Ben had meant what he'd said. And this time Ben would be out to kill him!

When?

He pulled the stud away from the pool. His lips were dry. He wanted a drink, wanted it badly. But he couldn't bring himself to belly down for it . . . he didn't want to die that way.

He walked back, leading the chestnut. His glance drifted across that silent, weathered building line. A board cracked in the hot sun. He jerked and went still, his gaze narrowing against the glare from the hills.

The chestnut threw up his head and nickered questioningly. There was no answer. But Mel knew that somewhere another cayuse was picketed, perhaps with Ben's hand stilling any answering sound.

The grim game of cat and mouse, he thought bleakly, and a savage anger glittered in his eyes. He felt like stepping clear of the stud and calling to Ben. But he knew Ben would come at him in Ben's own good time. . . .

He saw a wooden cross on the hill behind the windowless building which was all that was left of the Hide and Tallow Saloon. A footpath led up a slope to an outhouse perched on the crest; Mel could see clear through the abandoned bar, out the back door, to where the trail began.

The grave was at the other end of the ridge.

Mel tied the stud to the rail in front of the saloon and walked slowly through the bar, catching a glimpse of himself in the cracked bar mirror. He stepped out the back door and saw the first signs that someone else was there, or had been there very recently — there were fresh horse droppings in the yard.

He walked on. He went up the slope, momentarily expecting to hear Ben call, taunt him, before he fired. His face felt hot but the back of his neck was cold.

He turned left, away from the sagging shack on the ridge, and stopped by the lone grave. He stood very still, trying to remember the boy who was buried there and finding only a fuzzy memory.

The name on the headboard was:

ROBERT RAWLINS
Born July 2, 1851
Died June 7, 1876
He Came Where He Wasn't Wanted.

He forgot Ben, thinking of his kid brother and of happier days on Stirrup, when it had been a man's ranch — and home.

He didn't hear Ben step around a corner of the outhouse and stand in front of it. But Ben's hard voice reached him, jerked him back to the present.

"Figgered you'd come here, kid, after you left Manassas Smith."

Mel turned slowly. Ben faced him, fifty feet away, a gaunt, cold figure, his hand hooked slightly above his gun.

Deep frustration crawled through Mel and thickened his voice. "He's my brother, Ben. Buried here. What else could I do?"

"You could have ridden on, kid, like I told yuh." Ben shook his head. "You can't help him now. You should have ridden clear —"

"Ben! We rode a hard trail together. I thought you were a man who remembered a good turn."

"I remembered, kid. But I work for pay!

And you were warned!"

Mel's glance lifted past Ben to the hot hills hemming in this ghost town. So this is where it ends, he thought. Beside Bob's grave.

He took a long harsh breath. "Ben — I'm going back. You won't stop me!"

"You were never that good!" Ben said. He said it coldly, confidently.

"I'm going back," Mel repeated. "I want another look at that grave in the mission cemetery. I want to find out who is buried there."

For the first time Ben reacted. He stiffened, his hand jerking slightly. "Kid! Get out of here! Don't ever try to —"

Glass jangled suddenly in the hot still air as someone in the building below jammed a rifle muzzle through a pane.

Ben moved with the sound. In that first shocked moment he had to make a decision whether to turn toward the sound of breaking glass, or to kill Mel. That moment of uncertainty cost him his life.

Mel felt Ben's bullet go past his face. He shot twice. Ben jerked back, fell hard. He turned over once and tried to reach his gun which had fallen out of his hand. Then he collapsed, face down, in the hot sand.

Mel turned swiftly, expecting trouble

from the buildings below the ridge. He saw the blued muzzle of a rifle jutting out of the window of the top floor of the Reynolds House, targeting him. The cold even voice from somewhere behind it warned: "Drop that gun, mister. I can put two slugs in you before you turn around."

Mel dropped his Colt. He waited on the ridge, while the rifle remained on him. Then his eye caught the man who came around the corner of the building line. *Two of them,* he thought, and shot a quick glance toward the rifleman again. He couldn't see the man, but a curl of bluish cigarette smoke drifted out through the broken panes.

The man coming up the slope was a small, wiry man with a worried face. He was in his forties, but he looked older. He was wearing nondescript clothes, and he might have been any drifter heading for the Mexican border.

He held a Colt on Mel as he stooped quickly and picked up Mel's gun. He thrust it in his waistband, made a short gesture to the rifleman below. The rifle withdrew.

He walked slowly over to Ben's body, looked down at it. He waited, facing Mel, until his partner appeared on the footpath below. The man came up to join them, a taller, lanky man some years younger than the wiry saddle tramp.

He knelt beside the body and turned him over, smiled bleakly, and turned to Mel.

"Ben Stoll! You're pretty fast with that Colt, Mel. But I never expected to see the day you and Ben would wind up like this!"

Mel lifted his hands slightly from his sides, let them fall back. "You know about me and Ben?"

The other nodded. He came up, walking slowly, and pointed his rifle carelessly at Bob's grave. "We know about him, too."

"If you knew Bob," Mel said quietly, "then you know he was my brother."

"We figured that," the sandy-haired man said. "He was a better man than you, any day."

A tight smile crimped Mel's mouth. "I won't argue the point, mister. Not as long as that rifle is in your hands, anyway."

"I'm hanging onto it," the rifleman said levelly. "Fred and me thought you were with Ben Stoll. Figured both of you worked for that bunch in Manoas."

There was an unmistakable contempt in the tall man's voice that gave Mel a clue to where they stood in this matter. He measured them with narrowing gaze. They looked like drifters; the kind who would be hanging around the Oasis. But something set them apart. There was a sureness about them, a quiet understanding between them, that identified them as a long-working team.

"Ben and I parted company three months ago," he said. "Ben was a man on the move. He didn't like staying any place too long. I — well, I kinda had enough of it. So I went back home — to Stirrup."

He searched their faces, expecting some reaction. But the sandy-haired man's face was bland, and Fred, the wiry partner, was calmly chewing on a bit of cut plug.

"That's what brought me down here to Manoas," he said harshly. "Stirrup was a big spread. There was little left when I got back. Stock was gone, my father dead. Some of the old hands had been killed in the raids — the others had drifted out of the country."

"What brought you down here?" The sandy-haired man asked the question calmly, casually.

"My brother."

"Bob?"

Mel shook his head. "Hump. I got a letter asking me to meet him here —" He bit off his words, looked from the rifleman to the other. "Let's change sides, fellers," he suggested grimly. "Who are you?"

The sandy-haired man shrugged. "Fair enough." He took out his wallet, flipped it open. Mel glimpsed a gold star pinned to the inside flap.

"Border Patrol," the man said. "I'm Sandy McLain. This jasper with the worried look is my partner, Fred Humes."

Mel licked his lips. "The law?"

"You sound uneasy." McLain grinned.

"I haven't been too friendly with it," Mel answered shortly.

"Yeah." Sandy nodded. "We saw the dodger on you. Wanted for helping a gunslinger by the name of Ben Stoll break out of jail in a town called Tenejo." He glanced at Ben's body, and his eyebrows lifted. "You helped Ben break out of jail. And now you killed him."

Mel made a sharp gesture. "Don't make too much of it, feller. I didn't want to kill Ben. But he trailed me here. He was out to kill me."

"Why?"

"Ben was never a man to duck a job," Mel said bleakly. "He was a gunfighter, and his gun was for hire. Whoever had bought his gun wanted me killed."

"Someone in Manoas?"

"Reckon." Mel eased his hands down. "I came down here looking for Hump. I found his grave in Manoas — in the mission cemetery."

Sandy frowned. He looked at his partner, then back to Mel. "We got a letter from your brother Bob in the Corpus Christi office. Didn't tell us much; just that he had stumbled onto something here that we ought to look into. Something about smuggling that was going on through Manoas. Asked us to meet him in this old gold town of Tallow. But he was dead by the time we got here."

"Smuggling?" Mel made a wry face. "I didn't know about any smuggling. What I'm after are the men who smashed Stirrup."

"A big order," Sandy pointed out dryly.

Fred got rid of part of his chaw. "What you going to do now, feller?"

"Am I free to choose?"

Humes grinned. "Shore. Far as we're concerned, you're even with the law, for killing Ben."

"I didn't kill Ben to make up for getting him out of jail," Mel snapped. "I was with Ben when they railroaded him into that cell. The charge they hung on him was a lie. I didn't like to see a man framed — so I helped him out."

Sandy chuckled. "Ben must have gotten a kick out of that, Mel. He had killed half a dozen men before the Tenejo frame-up. He was wanted in Cochise County for murder and stage robbery, and in Taos for more of the same."

Fred wiped his chin with the back of his hand. "Ben was no Robin Hood —"

"He played square with me," Mel muttered. He was thinking that sometimes that was all a man had to go on. "I killed Ben because he came gunning for me — and for no other reason."

"You've got a curious sense of honesty," Humes observed. "We gave you an out. A lot of men would have jumped at it."

"I liked Ben," Mel repeated stubbornly. He walked over to the body. "I'd like to bury him."

"There's a shovel in the shed next to the saloon," Sandy said. "I'll get it for you."

Mel wiped the sweat from his face. Sandy and Fred were in the shade, watching. Sandy was smoking a thin cheroot.

Mel finished shoveling the last of the earth on Ben's grave and stuck the shovel into the ground at the head of it. He walked over to the two lawmen. They had been discussing something between them, but he had not been close enough to hear what they said.

"Do I get my gun back?"

Humes nodded. He slipped it from under his belt, handed it to Mel. "You figuring to ride north?"

Mel shook his head. "I'm riding back." There was a stubborn slant to Rawlins' jaw. "I came to Manoas to find out what happened to Bob and Hump. I found out. Now I want to know who killed them, and why."

Sandy stretched lazily. "We got somewhat the same idea, Mel." He got to his feet. "Come on. We've got something to show you."

Mel followed them down the slope, beyond the spring, to an old cistern and a sagging shed in a clearing. Two horses were picketed here.

Sandy reached in his saddle bag and brought out a rolled dodger. He flattened it out against the uncomplaining animal's flank. "Take a look at it," he told Mel. "Notice anything?"

Mel frowned. It was a poster of the Faraday Kid, with a $1000 reward for his delivery, dead or alive, to the sheriff of Pocano County. It was a head and shoulders profile shot of the Kid, a hard-jawed man in a black hat.

Mel shook his head. "I never ran into the Kid," he said.

"You shore have," Sandy grinned. "You're the Kid!"

Mel fell back a step, his eyes narrowed and hard. "You know who I am!" he snapped. "I told you. I'm not going to be hauled in on a fake dodger —"

"Easy, boy," Humes said. "That ain't the idea. We know you're not the Kid."

Sandy rolled the poster and slipped it back into his saddle bag. He turned to Mel. "We know the Kid's not within two hundred miles of Manoas. But you look like him. It ain't a good picture of the Kid, but you look a lot like that picture on the dodger. Now think about it, feller. Ben Stoll came after you to kill you. If you show up in Manoas, and Ben doesn't come back, they'll know what happened. Next time you won't have the chance Ben gave you."

"I'll take that chance!" Mel said.

"Let's cut the odds a little," Sandy suggested. "If you rode back as the Faraday Kid, it would throw them off. Up to now they've probably figured you as a prying stranger who had to be gotten rid of. So they sent Ben after you. Going back as the Kid, you might be able to talk your way into Ben's place —"

"Ben knew who I was," Mel pointed out grimly.

"Ben's dead."

"It's possible he told the men who hired him."

"It's possible," Sandy agreed soberly. "But it's still a chance, any way you look at it. And you might get by with it."

Mel took a long breath. "It's worth the gamble." He was thinking that Carl Spencer would be surprised to see him back. "How do we do it?"

Sandy patted his saddle bag. "Me and Fred are too well known to work under-cover. I've been in Manoas before. So I'll ride down into town and post this dodger on the Oasis wall. I've got another I'll tack up somewhere else. I'll stay in town just long enough to make a showing; then I'll leave. About sundown, you ride in. You take it from there, Mel."

Mel made a face. "It's worth a try."

Humes said quietly: "We've found out enough to know that they're smuggling Chinese in from Tampico. We think they come off a ship called the Hurricane. But we don't know who's behind it — when they land them — or where they take them. That's what we want to find out."

"That's what we hope you can find out," Sandy put in bluntly. "We'll give you all the help we can. But you'll be the sitting duck, Mel."

Mel nodded. "With one difference, Mc-Lain." His eyes had a cold, flat look in them. "I can shoot back!"

Chapter IX

Sandy McLain rode into Manoas in the afternoon. He stopped by the Oasis and, ignoring the stares of the redhaired gunslinger lounging on the porch, found an old rusty nail on the wall near the door and pinned the Kid's picture on it.

He stepped back and surveyed it. The redhaired gunman came over, his thumb hooked carelessly in his belt, and read the poster. His eyes narrowed, and he thumbed his hat back on his head.

"The Faraday Kid? Worth a thousand American pesos, eh?"

"On the hoof," Sandy said.

"Figger the Kid's down in this part of the country?" Turk asked.

"He might be looking for a boat to Tampico," Sandy replied. He turned and went down to his horse and rode away.

Turk studied the Kid's profile for a long moment; then he began to chuckle. He went inside the saloon and came back out with Carl Spencer.

The Oasis owner read the dodger while he chewed the soggy end of his cigar. "Close enough to be him," he admitted. "If we didn't know better . . ."

Sandy rode down to the Smith Brothers stables and pulled up in the yard. He waited until Manassas shuffled out to him.

"Howdy," Smith greeted him gruffly.

Sandy dismounted. "Won't be staying long," he said. "How much for water, feed and a rub-down?"

"One dollar — silver." Smith's voice was truculent.

He took the bridle and headed up the scarred ramp, and Sandy followed him inside the barn.

Smith turned and made a quick motion. "The Hurricane was in here yesterday. Hove to for about two hours. Captain Bremem came ashore alone and went into the Sea Horse, like he always does." Smith's voice had a dry humor. "Bremem didn't stay long this time. Ran into trouble with a stranger name of Mel Rawlins —"

"Then it was you who sent Rawlins to Tallow?"

Manassas grinned. "Good man to have on yore side, Sandy." The next thought brought a worried look to his face. "Ben

Stoll was headed yore way, too. Way I figgered it, he was after Mel."

"Ben found him," Sandy muttered. "Ben's dead."

Manassas shifted the subject. "The Hurricane's out there, Sandy. She's anchored about ten, twelve miles out —"

"Waiting for the fog?" Sandy's voice was cold.

"Maybe. I think they're running scared this time. If they get wind of trouble, they'll run."

"I had to come," Sandy muttered. "They must have been expecting me. I usually drop by this time of the year."

"You leaving right away?"

"Before sundown." He took the second dodger from among several others in his saddle bag. "Looks like Rawlins, doesn't it?"

Manassas squinted. "Some." He looked up quickly. "You don't mean —"

"No." Sandy cut him off. "But Rawlins is going to be the Kid for a few days."

"A decoy?"

Sandy shrugged.

Smith walked to the door and looked out. He turned, his voice distant. "He ain't a fool. And he's tough. But —"

"You like him?"

"I liked Bob Rawlins, too," Smith said. He sounded regretful. "But I never cottoned to the big one."

"He's dead."

Manassas showed stubs of teeth in a crooked grin. "That's what Mel's gonna find out. Or is he?"

Sandy nudged the oldster. "Keep out of it, Manassas. If they ever get wind of what you're doing —" He didn't finish. A rider had turned into the yard, was riding slowly toward the ramp.

Sandy showed himself in the doorway, looked back to Smith. "A rub-down will put some of the ginger back in him, Smith. I'll be by in about an hour —"

He walked down the ramp and glanced briefly at the newcomer. He kept walking, his face showing no sign of recognition. But his lips were pulled back against his teeth as he reached the street.

Neal Boone! Manoas seemed to have become the gathering spot for some of the worst outlaws in Texas.

He walked up the steep, winding road and paused in front of the Sea Horse. He had the second poster tucked under his arm as he went inside.

A Mexican couple with two small children were having dinner at one of the tables. Three fishermen were playing cards, gambling for the bottle of wine on the table. There was no one at the bar.

Tobey came over to greet McLain. "Checkup time again, Mr. McLain?" His tone was affable.

McLain nodded. He scratched idly, laying the dodger on the bar. "Have a chore to do, Tobey. I'll need a tack hammer and some nails. I'd like to put this up on your wall, if you don't mind?"

Tobey spread the dodger out and looked at it. A guarded look tightened the skin around his eyes. "Sure." He ducked under the counter and found an old hammer with one claw missing. More digging around produced a few rusty nails. "This do?"

"Do fine," Sandy answered.

Tobey studied the poster.

Sandy asked casually: "See this gent around here recently?"

"You looking for him?"

"Me?" Sandy shook his head. "I'm no bounty hunter, Tobey. My job's patrolling the border. Sheriff up in Idalgo County knew I was making a trip down here and asked me to put a couple of these up in town."

"You got another one?"

"Yeah. Nailed that one by the Oasis door."

Tobey reached up and scratched his ear.

"The Faraday Kid? Heard about him, McLain. But what would a gunslinger like that be doing in this coast town?"

"Don't know," Sandy replied. "Between you and me, I don't think he's within two hundred miles of here."

He picked up the hammer, nails and poster and went outside. Loan was standing in the kitchen doorway when he left. She came over to where Tobey was standing.

"Who was he?"

"Border Patrol. You remember, don't you? His name's McLain."

"Oh!" She searched Tobey's face, but saw nothing to alarm her. "What did he want?"

"Nails and a hammer." Tobey frowned. "He's tacking a dodger on our wall."

Loan went outside. Sandy had just finished. She stepped close and read the poster, taking a long look at the hard face of the Kid.

"Afternoon, Miss Stevens," Sandy said politely.

She nodded, turned quickly away, and went inside. Sandy scratched his head. He went back to the bar and laid the hammer down. Loan had disappeared into the kitchen.

"Your girl took one look at the Kid's face," he said, "and ran back like she'd seen a ghost."

"Could be," Tobey answered laconically. He looked Sandy in the eye. "A man who could be the Faraday Kid was in here yesterday. He left Manoas this morning. He called himself Mel."

Sandy was surprised. "The Kid in Manoas? Well, I'll be hanged!"

"You don't have to be," Tobey growled. "I said this man looked like the Kid. I'm not saying he is. Anyway, he left town this morning."

McLain licked his lips. "I'll have a drink, Tobey. Double shot." He watched Tobey pour. "None of my business," he said, tight-lipped. "Way I hear it, this Kid's bad medicine. I got a wife and two kids back in Corpus Christi. It ain't my job to hunt gunslingers like the Kid." His grin was a bad attempt to make a joke of it. "I'm here to check on wetbacks, Tobey. I'll have to give those poor Mexican fishermen down on the beach a bad time for an hour or so —"

He pushed a half-dollar on the counter and finished his whiskey. "If the Kid should come back, the boys up at the Oasis are welcome to that thousand dollars,

Tobey. But they sure will have to earn it."

He went out and walked down to the beach, where he made a pretense of questioning frightened villagers while a swarm of wide-eyed children followed him around.

An hour later he came back up the road to the Smith stables, paid his bill and rode away. He didn't look back. When he was out of sight a hard-eyed rider from the Oasis checked his carbine, then followed on the same road. . . .

Mel Rawlins came to Manoas after dark. He rode into Smith's stable yard and dismounted, keeping his back to the chestnut. He waited until Smith appeared, holding a dim lantern.

"Back again?"

Mel nodded. He followed Smith into the barn. The old man took the chestnut and turned him into a vacant stall.

Mel kept his voice low. "I found Bob's grave, and dug another."

Smith said: "You were lucky." He dropped the board behind the chestnut, locking him in the stall. "There's a poster of the Faraday Kid on Tobey's wall. The other's at the Oasis."

Mel hid his surprise. So Manassas knew

more than he had let on.

"The hay's clean up in the loft," Smith reminded him. "And I sleep light. If you come in tonight, say one word: Chucka-walla. I got an awfully itchy trigger finger."

He took the lantern and went out. Mel stood in the doorway, the darkness thick around him. It was a clear night, and there was enough starshine to see by.

Sometimes, he thought, boldness was the only course left. He could walk into the Oasis as the Faraday Kid and take his chances that his bluff would work. Or he could ride out of Manoas tonight, and keep on riding. . . .

He went up the road, stopping for a moment in the shadows opposite the Sea Horse. A ship's lantern, hung on a nail by the door, gave him a glimpse of the poster.

The Sea Horse was quiet, and the thought came to Mel that Tobey was lucky to make a living there, judging by the amount of business he seemed to have. He had a moment's brief wonder as to what kept this man here, a Yankee Puritan buried in a small Mexican fishing village on the Gulf.

He walked on, pausing again in the bend above the Sea Horse. He could see over the peaked roof, out to the dark stretch of the sea. Somewhere on the horizon a reddish star seemed to dip and roll. He closed his eyes, and when he opened them he saw it clearly for an instant. Then it faded again.

He kept walking. He went up toward the Oasis, and he could hear rough voices before he came to it. At least, he thought cynically, Carl Spencer was doing a thriving business.

He cut across the ridge, and five minutes later he stood in front of the big oak doors of the mission. They were open, and he could see inside the dim interior. Candles flickering in front of the altar gave him a creepy feeling.

He took off his hat and went inside. There was no one in the place except an old woman, her head covered by a black shawl. She was kneeling in front of the statue of St. Joseph, silent in her meditation.

He turned and looked back, out through the wide doorway. The town below the ridge was lost in the darkness.

The old woman was oblivious to his entrance. Mel walked down the aisle between the hard wooden benches and found a side door leading to a patio.

A colonnaded walk led along the side of the mission to a small adobe building in back. He followed it, his boots making a flat sound on the flagstones, disturbing the silence.

He saw a light against the high narrow window, went around to the door and knocked.

The door opened. Father Pinone was short, round and cherubic. He was wearing steel-rimmed spectacles, and his soft brown eyes blinked a welcome to Mel.

"*Señor* . . . come in, please."

In his hand he was holding a book which he had obviously been reading. Now he laid it on a small oak table as he offered Mel a chair.

Mel declined. "Thank you, Father." His voice was stiff and a little uncomfortable.

"I'm Father Pinone," the priest said. "You are a stranger here?"

"Yes. I was up here yesterday. Perhaps you saw me then. I came to visit a grave."

"Yes. I remember." Father Pinone nodded soberly. "I saw you from the colonnade — I was on my way to the altar. You were with the *Señorita* Stevens."

"She joined me." Mel was silent a moment, trying to shape his words. "I came here tonight because of that grave, Father Pinone. My name's Mel Rawlins."

"Yes?" It was obvious that the priest did not know the connection between Mel and the man buried in the mission cemetery. He stood waiting, smiling.

"The man buried there is my brother," Mel said, "Hump Rawlins."

"Oh!" The smile vanished from Father Pinone's face. He seemed genuinely distressed. "I understand now. A terrible way to die — far from home —"

"You saw him?"

"Your brother? No . . . no, I didn't." Father Pinone's smooth brow puckered. "I said a prayer at the grave. But the coffin was already sealed. I — you must understand, *Señor* Rawlins, I didn't know him. When I was approached by *Señorita* Stevens concerning the burial of your brother here, I was very surprised. But I was told he was a Catholic, that it was where he would want to be buried." He made a quick gesture. "If there has been some mistake . . ."

"Perhaps," Mel said. "You did not see the dead man?"

"No." Father Pinone's round face was puzzled.

"Was there anyone at the funeral besides Miss Stevens?"

"Some of the fishermen from the beach, *señor.* And one man . . . a big man . . ."

Mel's voice was harsh, quick. "Can

127

you describe him?"

"I saw him only that once, *señor*." The priest groped back in his memory. "He was tall — taller and bigger than you even. And he seemed to have a hump on his back. His shoulders . . . they were round, as though he had carried a heavy load too long. Not much else, I'm afraid. . . . Oh, yes. When he smiled, just once, I saw a tiny white scar at the corner of his mouth."

Mel stood very quiet. He heard Father Pinone say something else, but it didn't register. The small, bare room was deathly still, and inside himself he felt dead.

". . . Can I get you something, *Señor* Rawlins?" The sharp concern in the priest's voice reached him finally. "Some port, perhaps? You seem ill."

"No, I'm all right." Mel pulled himself together. "Thanks very much, Father."

"Is there any more I can do for you?"

"Not now. Perhaps some day I can do something for you," Mel said. He walked to the door.

"Your brother — will you want to remove his body?"

A faint, tight grin showed around the edges of Mel's hard mouth. "No. We'll let him stay where he is, Father. He couldn't be buried in a better place."

Chapter X

He stood outside the mission doors and pondered his next move. He knew what faced him if he stayed in Manoas. And knowing this, he eyed the lights of the town below the ridge with cold and bitter eyes.

Ben had warned him. But he had been stubborn, and he had wound up killing Ben. Sandy McLain and his partner had their own points of view, shaped by their calling. But he had known Ben Stoll in a way they never would. No man, he reflected, is all bad. And Ben was a man shaped by his times — and the times in Texas, ten years after Lee surrendered to Grant, were violent times.

Mel had seen too much of Reconstruction law to have any respect for it. And he was not quite sure he trusted McLain and Fred Humes, or cared much for their help.

What he had to do in Manoas he would have to do alone.

He walked back to the Oasis, paused just

long enough to pull the dodger down off the wall, and went inside.

He spotted Tane and his crew at a poker table. The Navajo was in a far corner by himself, his face buried in his arms. He seemed to be asleep. The sheepmen were gone, but the miners were still celebrating, and the three percentage girls were with them. The piano player had the night off.

Mel walked to the bar. There was only one man at the rail, a tough-looking Mexican, brooding over his beer.

Out of the corner of his eyes he saw Tane's bunch become quiet. . . . The red-headed gunman who had been taunting the Navajo the night before turned around in his chair and leaned forward.

Mel waited until the bartender came over. Then he slapped the poster on the bar. His voice was rough. "Who's the joker who tacked this up outside?"

The bartender saw the bright glitter in Mel's eyes and knew a dangerous man when he faced one. He gulped, and shot a quick glance at the card players. "I didn't see it, mister —"

"The name's Faraday," Mel snarled, "same as on this dodger." He shoved the poster under the bartender's nose. "I want to know who's looking for me!"

Turk pushed his chair back and got up. He came toward the bar, moving with the slow, flatfooted stride of a man looking for trouble.

"Reckon I am, Kid." He raised his voice above the noise of the miners. "Me, Turk Williams! That thousand dollars looks pretty good to me!"

Mel turned on his elbow. There was no one at his back, and only the Mexican at the bar. The man saw the look in Mel's eyes, smiled thinly and put both hands on the counter, palms flat.

Mel stepped clear of the rail and faced Turk, recognizing the redheaded, turkey-necked man with the cast in his eye.

"It comes high," Mel said bleakly. "You ain't good enough to earn it."

"I ain't playing muscle games," Turk sneered. "I don't need a strong arm to take you, Kid. Just a —"

"Big mouth!" Mel snapped, saw a glare of anger leap up in Turk's eye, and drew. He shot from the hip, a double report that doubled Turk, twisted him around, sent him sprawling. He turned face downward and reached a freckled hand past his mouth, and blood stained the back of his hand. He shuddered once and went still.

No one made any sudden move. Mel

turned as the door of Carl's office jerked open. Carl himself was framed in it. A cigar jutted from his bulldog jaws. He stood very quietly, his gaze shuttling from the smoking gun in Mel's hand to Turk's body.

"Anyone else in here planning to make an easy thousand bucks?" Mel taunted.

A tall, cold-eyed man loomed up behind Carl Spencer. He started to push the Oasis owner, but Carl put out a hand. The man relaxed, his eyes on Mel, watchful as a big cat's.

Carl came to the bar, jerked a finger at the bartender for service. He turned to Mel.

"What's eating you, Kid?"

Mel's eyes had a suspicious stare. "You running a bounty hunting outfit?"

Carl reached out and pulled the dodger to him. He glanced at it, then looked into Mel's face. "So you're the Faraday Kid? Why didn't you say so?"

"You didn't ask me."

Carl took it. Too readily, Mel thought. He turned away from the rail and walked over to Turk's body. He said indifferently: "Couple of you boys bring Turk out to the shed in back. We'll bury him tomorrow." His wave included everybody. "The drinks are on the house, boys."

The Navajo got to his feet, as though a bell had rung in his head, calling him. He pushed in alongside Mel, shouldering a raw-boned, tough-faced man who reacted as though he had been brushed by the plague. He jerked back and his hand fell to his gun, while his eyes blazed.

"Get away from the bar, Chief! *I* don't drink with Injuns!"

The Navajo turned. His flat face held no visible emotion, but he took a step toward the man.

The gunslinger lifted his Colt. "Go ahead, Chief. Try it, an' I'll splatter you all over this room!"

Mel put a hand on the Navajo's shoulder. "The Chief's drinking!" he said. His voice was low, quiet. "And I'd think twice before I tried to splatter anybody around."

The gunman's gaze dropped to the muzzle leveled at his stomach. Mel had drawn unobtrusively and was holding his gun down against his hip.

Carl pushed in between them. "Sully, give the boys a hand with Turk. You can have your drinks later."

The Chief stepped up to the rail, brushing contemptuously against the gunman. Sully quivered. But he turned away and went to join the men lifting Turk's body.

The dark-faced gunman who had been in Carl's office drifted over. Carl introduced them. "Neal Boone. He's from your part of the country, Kid. Kansas, isn't it?"

Neal nodded coldly. He made no other acknowledgment, but his pale eyes studied Mel carefully, the way a gunfighter studies another of the breed.

They had a couple of drinks; then Mel asked Carl if he could see him in his office. Carl nodded.

They went to the office, and Mel closed the door behind him. Carl walked to his desk. Mel's flat voice stopped him.

"I had to kill him, Carl."

The Oasis owner turned, his thighs against the desk. "Turk?"

"Ben Stoll!"

Carl's face seemed to bunch around his cigar. He moved to his chair and sat down slowly. "I don't know any Ben Stoll."

"Like fun you don't!" Mel rasped. "You sent Ben out to kill me. Why?"

Carl shook his head. "Don't know anyone named Ben Stoll, Kid. If he —" He went still, his eyes flat and emotionless as Mel drew his Colt. "You won't get past that door, Kid — if you shoot!"

"I'll take the chance," Mel said. He was

bluffing, but he wanted to make it stick.

Carl's face was like putty. "What you after, Kid?"

"Ben didn't know I was the Faraday Kid," Mel said. "He rode after me to kill me this morning. But Ben made one big mistake. He always was too sure of himself. He stepped out in front of me, instead of in back —"

"I didn't send Ben," Carl said hoarsely. "I don't give the orders here."

"You told me that before," Mel recalled. "You also told me to come back today. I'm back!"

Carl gulped. "I haven't got an answer for you, Kid." He shrank back in his chair as Mel cocked his Colt. "Easy with that trigger, Kid! Give me until tomorrow. If you still want in —"

"It was Ben's idea in the first place," Mel cut in harshly. "That's why I came to Manoas. Ben's dead. Maybe the boss can use another gun."

Carl nodded quickly. "Sure, Kid — sure." He got up, his legs a little shaky. "Let's drink on it, Kid."

Mel shook his head. "Two's my limit." He eased the hammer back and shoved his Colt into the holster. "I'll be back to-morrow."

He walked out, stopped by the bar long enough to pick up the dodger still on the counter. He tore it into quarters and tossed the pieces over the bar.

Carl waited in his doorway. The color came slowly back into his face. After a while he made a motion that brought Sully and Neal Boone to his office. They went inside, and he closed the door.

The Navajo had drifted back to his table. He put his head down on his thick arms and began to snore. . . .

Chapter XI

The Mexican *cantina* down on the beach
was small and dingy. The low roof made
Mel feel like ducking his head as he entered. The heavy smell of fried beans and
chili was strong, mingled with smoke and
sour mash.

But it was the only eating place in
Manoas besides the Sea Horse. And he
hadn't wanted to see Loan tonight, or push
Tobey.

The café was not more than twenty feet
long, and the tables were crowded. A
stocky young Mexican sweated behind the
bar. The customers, in their own element
here, were noisy. After the first curious ap-
praisal, they ignored the tall stranger.

Mel found a table in the corner. He
could see the front door, and the kitchen
opening was at his elbow, five feet away. An
older, heavier replica of the young man behind the bar popped in and out of the
kitchen, carrying food to the tables.

Mel gave the man his order. He had eaten here before and was no longer a stranger to the owner.

"*Si, señor.*" Tomaso mopped sweat from his oily face. He turned to his son behind the bar. "Bring the *señor* a bottle of tequila, Jose. Pronto . . . pronto. . . ."

He disappeared into the kitchen. Jose brought the tequila and a glass. Mel waited. He was expecting trouble . . . and he knew it would come through the front door.

He was halfway through his meal when Neal Boone came in.

The gunman was tall enough to have to duck as he entered. He came inside and paused, his eyes seeking Mel in the dimly-lighted café. There was only one big oil lamp hanging near the bar, and the smoke hung in a thick haze in the room.

He saw Mel and turned to him, his teeth startlingly white against the dark skin of his face.

Slowly Mel laid down his knife and fork. Boone said coldly: "Finish yore meal, Kid. I ain't in that much of a hurry."

The chatter in the room died away. The men at the table between Boone and Mel looked uneasy. Tomaso came out of the kitchen, his face white as a sheet. He walked slowly to where his son was standing.

Sully appeared in the kitchen doorway, a cocked Colt in his hand. He turned slightly to face Mel, an implacable hatred in his eyes.

"I ain't that patient, Neal!" His voice was harsh and final.

The desperation in Mel did not show in his face or his voice. He ignored Sully, spoke to Neal. "You're taking the hard way to make a thousand dollars, fella."

Sully guffawed. "We got you whipsawed, Kid! You ain't got the chance of a snowball in hell, an' you know it! Get up! Or take it —"

He jerked, a startled look flashing across his face. His mouth opened, but no sound came out of it. His gun went off, and across the room one of the fishermen flinched. . . . The men between Boone and Mel dove for the floor.

Sully plunged across the room as though he had been shoved. He rammed into Tomaso, who stood frozen, and Mel had time for a glimpse of the knife in Sully's back. . . . Then he was lunging up, spilling the small table.

Neal's first shot scoured a gash across his ribs. He got in two shots while Neal, shifting, stumbled over one of the men on the floor. Neal spun around and fell backward.

A thick figure appeared briefly in the kitchen doorway, waved to Mel, and disappeared. No one else saw him. All eyes were on Sully and Neal.

Mel backed into the kitchen, whirled, and stumbled over the cook who was crawling toward the door. The man had been slugged, and there was blood in his eyes.

The back door was open. Mel plunged out. A thick hand clamped down on his gun arm, spun him around. A guttural voice said one word: "Come!"

The strong fingers let go of his arm. Mel turned and followed the Navajo into the night.

No one in the *cantina* cared enough to follow them. The Chief knew his way in the dark; like some big prowling cat, he led Mel to a point behind the Smith stables.

"You smart — you ride now!" he grunted.

Mel's side burned. He hunkered down in the shadows, sucked in a harsh breath.

"I ain't that smart, Chief. Neither are you. If they find out you helped me, your hide won't be worth a plugged nickel."

The Navajo shrugged. "Me gotta die sometime. . . ."

Mel grinned. "Why, Chief? Why help me?"

The Navajo stood straight in the dark. He was dirty and unwashed, and the chicken feathers in his hair were ridiculous. But there was a certain dignity in the man. "I no like Crooked Mouth. An' you my friend."

He put a hand on Mel's shoulder. "They try again, Strong Arm. You smart . . . you ride tonight. . . ."

He was gone then, a shadow lost in the night. Mel waited awhile before heading for the stable yard.

He was in the darkness by the ramp when he heard the faint click of a gun hammer, and the warning sent a shock of remembrance racing through him. "Chuckawalla!" he said quickly, spinning against the barn wall.

There was a moment's uneasy silence. Then Smith's dry voice came from the darkness. "You came within a notch of sproutin' wings, Mel, or a tail. I ain't sure which."

Mel's voice was exasperated. "You ever sleep?"

"An' miss all the fun?" Smith chuckled.

"Most everythin' excitin' happens at night. Ever think of it? Whole world changes after the sun goes down. Sky changes. The sea is different. Town, too. Man who sleeps all night sees only half of life — the dull half."

"Philosopher in a manure pile," Mel said impatiently. He was feeling tired, and his side pained him.

"Better than a fool who deliberately sticks his head in a gun barrel." Smith's voice was stiff.

Mel walked toward the man. "Now, don't you get on your high horse, Smith. I got a bullet across my ribs, and it didn't put me in the proper mood for listening to a discourse on night life."

Smith grunted sympathetically. "Lucky it wasn't through yore head. Come on in."

Mel followed the sound of the man to the back door of a small shack where Smith lived. He felt his way inside and stood with his back to the wall as Smith closed the door. The odor of stale tobacco hung in the room. He heard the oldster move about, drawing a curtain across the one window. Then Smith scraped a match and lighted a candle in a tin can holder sitting on a corner shelf.

Smith motioned him to the bunk. Mel sat down on the edge, and Smith helped him get his bloody shirt over his head. Mel winced as Smith probed at the gash.

"Heard the shootin' down at the *cantina*," Smith remarked. "You like Mexican chow?" He was talking as he studied the gash under Mel's left arm. "Mexican cookin' is too hot for me."

"It was more than the cooking that was hot tonight," Mel admitted. He told Smith what had happened.

"Had you whipsawed, eh? And you got away with only this?" Smith's tone was mildly skeptical.

Mel hesitated. He didn't know how far he could go with this old codger, but after thinking it over, he decided there was no one in Manoas he could trust more.

"The Chief helped me out. You know, the big Navajo who bums drinks in the Oasis. He got Sully, and it gave me a chance to even up with Boone."

"The Chief?" Smith stood back and shook his head. "He's been in Manoas about five years. Drifted into town, drunk as a skunk, an' has managed to stay that way. Nobody knows where he sleeps. Nobody ever sees him eat. He shows up at the Oasis about openin' time, an' they generally have to sweep him out when they close."

He poured some water into a small basin and washed the blood away from the cut. "Ain't got anythin' but carbolic acid," he said. "If it's good enough for hosses, it oughta be good enough for you."

He spread some of the salve over the cut and grinned at the tears that came into Mel's eyes. "Stings, eh?"

"No," Mel gritted. "I'm just the emotional type."

He watched Smith tie a rough bandage around his ribs. He stood up, naked to the waist, and tried moving his left arm.

"You'll live," Smith grunted. He picked up Mel's bloodstained shirt.

"Burn it," Mel advised. "I've got a clean one in my bag. I'll put it on in the morning."

"You kin sleep here tonight," Smith said gruffly.

"The hayloft's fine," Mel said. "And I like the smell of the sea."

Smith shrugged. "Suit yoreself."

He walked to the candle, blew it out. His voice was kindly. "Sleep easy."

Mel walked to the door. "Thanks, Smith." He walked across the dark yard and went into the barn. His side hurt as he climbed the ladder to the loft. But the hay felt good under him. He placed his Colt near his head and lay back, listening to the distant pounding of the surf. After a few moments he fell asleep.

Chapter XII

Carl Spencer ignored the big man moving restlessly about the room. He was by the window of his upstairs bedroom, looking down on the roofs of Manoas, letting his thoughts run with the sea. It was morning, and he had not spent a restful night. . . . He had spent the early hours watching three graves being dug in the makeshift graveyard by the old factory.

He turned as the door opened and Tobey Hawkins came in. His jaws clamped down around his cigar, and he stood there, his manner defensive and defiant.

Tobey Hawkins closed the door behind him with a deliberateness that indicated a harshly controlled anger. He leaned back against it, his uncovered eye moving from Hump Rawlins, who had come to a stop by the wash stand, to Carl Spencer.

Spencer licked his lips around his cigar, spat it out. "The Hurricane's signaled twice, Tobey. Bremem's getting impatient."

"The devil with Bremem!" Tobey moved into the room, turning his attention to Hump. His eye had a cold, accusing glint.

"It's your turn," he said.

Hump wagged his head slowly. "No. We made a bargain, Tobey. I let you smash Stirrup."

"We would have done it anyway," Tobey said. "The spread was in our way. We made it fast and clean."

"It would have been harder without my help," Hump said. His voice was tight. "I could have gone to the law with what I knew."

Tobey shook his head. "You can't bargain now. It's too late for bargains."

"I can't face him! I'm not fast enough, Tobey! I wanted Mel killed! That was our agreement —"

"We lost four men," Tobey reminded him, "four good men."

"That's not my fault," Hump gritted. "I warned you about Mel."

Tobey looked at Carl. "Where's Tane and the rest of the boys?"

"Headed back for camp. Tane's getting things ready for the new bunch." He smiled bitterly. "If Bremem ever gets the word to come in."

"He'll come in," Tobey snapped. "He's

waiting to get paid for his cargo." He turned to Hump. "But I can't hold him off much longer. And I'm not going to break up this highly profitable business just because your brother is still alive. This time you get him!"

Hump stood adamant. "No." His voice was little more than a whisper. "All my life I've been bigger than Mel, but he always beat me. He could run faster, throw farther, jump higher. When we grew up he still beat me. I hated him. I hated him so much I married his girl." He laughed, a short, ugly laugh. "I married her, Tobey, but I didn't have her. You know what that means? I had nothing. . . ."

Tobey shrugged.

"That's why I was ready to throw in with you, Tobey. I wanted to smash Stirrup. I wanted to hurt Mel and to hurt Ruth. I didn't care who else I hurt." His voice was hoarse, unrepentant. "I still don't care."

"We lost four men," Tobey repeated harshly.

Hump lifted his head. "Lose four more!" he snarled. "We made an agreement —"

Tobey looked at Carl, then back to Hump. He knew human nature well enough to know he could not push this man further.

"We don't have anyone in town," he pointed out. "And we can't wait." He walked up to Hump, his voice growing more reasonable. "Look! You want your brother killed. I'll fix it so you can do it — in a way that will involve no risk."

Hump licked his lips. "How?" It was a whisper of defeat.

Tobey outlined what he had in mind. He went over it slowly, filling in every detail.

Hump licked his lips. "You sure he'll be there?"

"He'll be there."

Hump turned to Carl. The Oasis owner shook his head. "Count me out," he said glumly. "I didn't make any deal like that. I don't care how you get rid of him. We've got to unload soon. And I don't feel too easy about the border lawman, McLain. He's no fool. I sent Chris after him, to make sure he didn't turn back."

"This is our last job, Carl," Tobey said. "I think we've pushed our luck far enough. I'm telling Bremem we're through, after this load."

Carl shrugged. "What'll I tell Hump's brother when he comes around?"

"Tell him he's in with us."

"He'll want to know about *El Patrone*."

"Tell him I'm out at the desert camp.

Ask him to wait around. Say I'll be back tonight. Tell him anything. But keep him downstairs."

Carl nodded.

Tobey looked at Hump. The big man was rubbing his knuckles, a faraway look in his eyes.

"Cauldron Point," Tobey said. A flicker of a sardonic smile glinted in his eye. "Good place for it to come to a boil between you, eh, Hump?"

Hump turned away. Tobey looked at Carl, winked, and went out.

Loan Stevens came to the door of the Sea Horse. Tobey had gone out, and she was alone, and there never was any business in the early morning hours.

She leaned against the support, feeling the sun warm her face. She was wearing Levi's and a faded shirt, and there was nothing about her to suggest any change.

But she had changed. Or rather, the world about her had changed. It had lost its security, its familiarity — it had become suddenly bigger than this small coastal village and as uncertain as the sea.

She had never felt like a prisoner before, but she was a prisoner here, and now she knew it.

She had been used, been lied to. She had been a pawn to lure a man to his death, to deceive him.

She turned back into the house for her fishing pole and bait. The sea had always been friendly, and when she felt confused and afraid, there was a place to which she went.

But there was no eagerness in her this morning. She walked slowly past the fishing shacks, nodding hello to the women mending nets. The children ran to her, and she felt around in her pockets for the hard candy she usually carried with her. She shook her head, and saw the disappointment on the small brown faces.

She followed the shoreline. She kept in close to the jutting cliffs, wading around rocks. The sea rolled in here and smashed against the outlying reefs and washed in white froth toward her.

Eventually she came out to the tiny cove where Mel Rawlins had first come upon her. This was her favorite fishing spot. She climbed Old Woman, the big, mussel-grown rock that thrust into the surf, and pulled a small can of worms from her pocket.

Mel Rawlins found her there.

She was dreaming, looking out over the

blue, sparkling water, her pole held loosely. Her knees were drawn up to her chin, and fish were a long way from her thoughts.

"You look as pretty, but not as sassy, as when I first saw you," he said.

His voice shocked her. Her pole slid from her knees and clattered off the rock. She turned, her face pink as that of a schoolgirl caught in her mother's powder jar.

Mel was back against the cliff, in a little gouged-out pocket where he was invisible to anyone but the girl. He was building a smoke, his hat tilted back from his face.

She was not the girl of three days ago, sure of herself in her naïveté and un-touched emotionally by this man. She managed a weak, small question.

"How did you find me?"

"Followed you." He lighted the cigarette, dropped the match. "Saw you pass by and followed you. Got my feet wet, too."

"What do you want of me?" There was no fear in her voice.

"I want to get something straight," he said, "some thing you can tell me."

"I have nothing for you, Mr. Faraday Kid —"

"Cut it!" he said roughly. "You know I'm not the Kid, I'm Mel Rawlins, Hump's brother!"

Her voice was small. "What do you want to know?"

"Hump isn't dead, is he? He never was buried up in the mission cemetery?"

"How did you find out?"

"I guessed. I asked Father Pinone. I —" He frowned. "Come down here, Loan. I don't like talking up to you. And someone might see us."

She climbed down from the rock. Her bare feet left prints in the wet sand.

"Hump was with you when you buried someone in the mission yard," Mel said. "Father Pinone described my brother to me. Was it his idea to put his name on that headstone?"

She nodded weakly. "He showed up at the Sea Horse two weeks after the young man, the blond one —"

"Bob?"

"Yes. After Bob came. Tobey said he was an old friend of his. So I believed him when he told me someone was after him, wanted to kill him. He said he was tired of running. If I would go along with him to carry out a little scheme he had in mind, maybe you'd believe he was dead and go away. It sounded all right to me. I felt noble . . . a conspirator doing a good deed."

"Is Hump in Manoas now?"

"I haven't seen him in more than a week," she said. "But I think he was in the Sea Horse the night you arrived in Manoas. I didn't see him. . . ."

Mel discarded his cigarette. "I'll find him," he said. But he sounded miserable.

She put a hand on his arm in an instinctive gesture. "Mel — I was a girl two days ago. I'm twenty years old, but I was still a girl. I was happy here, fishing and cooking for Tobey, playing big sister to the little Mexican children. I lived in a little private world of my own, and the future was bright because Tobey told me so. He said some day he would have enough money to take me back East, where I would have servants and be driven around in a carriage. And I would meet men, men different from those who came to Manoas, men who read books."

Her smile was tremulous. "But life isn't lived in books, is it? And the present is more real than the future."

"I grew up knowing that," Mel answered. He said it quietly, for he understood this girl. "Today is all anyone has."

"Why does he hate you? Your own brother."

"I don't really know." He looked past her

to the combers breaking against the rocks, searching for an answer. "I could give you an explanation, but it might be the wrong one. It hurts, Loan. In a strange, sharp way, it hurts. I thought I knew Hump. I never really got close to Bob."

"Bob's dead?"

He nodded. "I found his grave — in Tallow."

"He was nicer, in some ways, than you," she said. Reaction sent a shiver through her. "I want to get out of here, Mel. I don't want Tobey's money, or his future. I want to get away from Manoas. What shall I do?"

"I don't know," he answered her.

She was close to him, her eyes wide, searching his hard face. Her lips parted. "I've never been this close to a man before," she said. "I've never felt the way I do now. But I know what it is, Mel. I love you —"

He kissed her. She was small and trusting in his arms and her lips were soft and unknowing. He felt her body quiver.

She pushed away. "Mel! Take me with you! Take me with you!"

He nodded. "When I leave, I'll take you with me, Loan — I'll take you home. . . ."

Chapter XIII

Sandy McLain came down the rocky slope to join his partner standing by the horses. He stuffed his field glasses into his saddle bag.

"Reckon there was only the one. Probably sent out to check on me."

"Mean-looking cuss," Fred said. He was chewing on a stem of grass. "He had you covered when I snuck up on him." He grinned. "All I said was, 'What you doing, fella?' and he tried to shoot me."

"You want to bury him?" Sandy asked carelessly.

"Me?" Fred shook his head. "Too hot. And my hands are too tender."

Sandy glanced at the horny palms of his partner. "Like old leather," he grunted. "We'll let him lay."

He reached in his shirt pocket for the makings, found none and looked at Fred, who tossed him his sack of Bull Durham. Fred watched him build a cigarette.

"They signaled again last night," he said. "The Hurricane's out there, waiting to come in. What's holding them?"

Sandy shrugged. "Us, maybe. Or Mel." He scowled at his limp cigarette. "Think we can trust him, Fred?"

Fred's mouth had a sour twist. "Can he trust us, you mean. We set him up like a sitting duck, remember?"

"He was a sitting duck anyway," Sandy snapped.

Humes nodded. "Either way, he was in trouble. But I kinda cottoned to him, Sandy. I liked what he said about Ben Stoll."

"A man can stick by his friends and still be a thief!" Sandy growled. But his voice lacked conviction. "He should have been in touch with us before this —"

"If he's still alive," Fred reminded him.

Sandy glanced sharply at him. "Yeah. Well, I'll wait until tonight. Then I'll try to sneak into town to see Smith."

"Give him a few more hours," Fred said. "He seemed a hard man to kill."

It was almost noon when Carl Spencer saw Mel walk into the Oasis. The place was deserted. One of the percentage girls was talking to the bartender. The other two were upstairs, packing. All three were leaving this afternoon, riding with Ken Murdy, who did the freighting into Manoas.

Mel paused for a quick look around. Carl gestured to him and Mel walked to the bar.

"Expected you sooner," Carl greeted him. He picked up the bottle at his elbow and turned to his office. Mel followed him. Inside, he waited while Carl found a couple of glasses and poured out drinks.

"I didn't think you'd be expecting me at all," Mel said.

Carl found a fresh cigar and bit into it. "Why? Because of last night?"

Mel frowned. "Something like that."

Carl made an expansive gesture. "Kid, I can't help it if Boone decided he could use that thousand-dollar reward. The boss was plenty sore when he found out."

"Sully, too," Mel said coldly. "Was the boss sore about him?"

Carl settled back in his chair and rolled his glass between his palms. "Sully and Boone made that fool play on their own, Kid. They're both dead. If you still want to take Ben's place here, you're in."

Mel considered this. It was too pat. He knew Hump was alive. And Hump would not be fooled by that Faraday Kid dodger.

If it was Hump who was running the show here, he had something up his sleeve.

"Sure," Mel agreed. "I want in. But I want to hear it from *El Patrone* himself. I like to deal direct."

"He'll be here," Carl promised. "He's busy right now. He's out at the desert camp with Tane. They're getting ready to pick up the new bunch tomorrow night."

Mel indicated only mild curiosity. "Desert camp?"

"Yeah." Carl dismissed it at once. "The boss'll tell you everything you want to know when he sees you. He promised he'd be in before sundown."

"Then I'll wait," Mel said. He finished his drink.

"I'll be with you in a few minutes," Carl said. "Pip, the bartender out there, will give you what you want. I've got a bit of book work I need to catch up on. Mind?"

Mel shook his head. "I'll be in the bar."

Coming out, he spotted the Chief in a far corner. The Navajo was asleep, his face on the table. Mel smiled. The Indian was like a cat. . . . He did his sleeping in the daytime and his prowling at night. He and Smith ought to get together, he thought.

The girl had gone back upstairs. Mel walked up to the bartender. But the balding, sour-faced man was no conversationalist. After evoking a few grunts, Mel asked for a pack of cards and retired to a corner to play solitaire.

Carl joined him late in the afternoon. A couple of down-at-the-heels miners looking for a grubstake drifted in. Carl went over to talk to them.

It was getting gray outside when an old Mexican came into the Oasis. He was wearing straw sandals, an old, moth-eaten serape, and a bewildered look. He saw Mel and shuffled over.

His smile was tentative, that of a man not sure of his reception. "You are the *Señor* Rawlins?"

Mel stiffened. He shot a quick glance at Carl, but the Oasis owner was busy with the two miners.

The Mexican had not waited for his answer. He was holding out a small cloth doll which he had furtively taken from inside his shirt.

Mel recognized the sad face immediately. Tipi. His hand reached out, clamped on the old Mexican's arm. "Where did you get that?"

"From the *Señorita* Stevens." He glanced around, his wrinkled face alarmed. "She say to tell you to meet her at Caul-

160

dron Point. Come right away —"

Mel nodded. He tucked the doll inside his shirt just as Carl turned away from the miners and came over.

The old Mexican was bobbing his head apologetically. "*Señor* — I was told to wait until I got ten pesos —"

Mel found a five-dollar gold piece and tossed it to him. Carl watched the old man head for the door.

"Who's the mummy?"

Mel thought quickly. "Somebody from the *cantina.* Claimed I owed money for the damages last night."

Carl's cigar jerked in his mouth. "Why, the dirty crooks! The boss paid for all damages!"

Mel was on his feet. Carl turned to him. "You're not leaving? The boss'll be here any minute now!"

"I'll be back." Mel's voice was careless. "Tell him to wait."

Carl watched him stride out, a thin gleam in his eyes. "You just think you'll be back!" he muttered. "This time, feller, your luck won't hold!"

Dusk shrouded Cauldron Point. The pounding of the surf below was faint, and the wind was off the sea, wet against Mel's face.

He had come with the dismal feeling that Loan might have broken with her foster father, Tobey, and run away. He could not imagine her parting with this silly little cloth doll for anything less urgent. But as he rode now wariness built up in him.

What did he know about this girl? A faint bitterness came to take away the pleasant taste of the afternoon. She had lied for Hump once before . . . maybe she had lied again.

He saw the animal up ahead just as the chestnut tossed his head and whinnied his greeting. The mare answered, jerking on her reins. She was tied to a small bush growing close to the edge of the point.

Mel looked for Loan, but he didn't see her. He kneed the chestnut ahead.

There was a knob of crumbly rock to the left of the mare, and if Loan was there, she might be waiting behind it. But at the last minute suspicion was too strong. . . . He had his hand on his Colt butt as he rode the stallion around the rock, perilously close to the edge of the cliff.

He saw the big man clearly. And something deeper than hatred held his hand. He said: "Hump!" And then a heavy report exploded in his head. He slumped over, and the rearing chestnut took the next bullet through the neck. It shuddered and lost its footing and went blindly over the edge. . . .

Hump looked down into the dark, swirling water breaking against the cliff below. The tide was in, and the current was strong around the point. He saw nothing. It was already too dark to see anything.

He heard a step behind him. He turned, his eyes searching the tall shadow coming up. "Well, it's done!" Intense relief was in his voice. "My brother won't be meddling in my life anymore!"

The man in the shadows said, "Fine, Hump." He fired twice. Hump took both slugs in the chest. He hadn't even seen the gun in the other man's hand.

The shock hammered him back. A bloody gurgle gushed out of him. Then he fell backward, into the dark, boiling sea below.

His killer waited a few moments, then turned and walked back to where he had hidden his cayuse. The mist was coming in fast as he rode back to Manoas.

Chapter XIV

Sandy McLain was dreaming. It wasn't a pleasant dream, and he rolled over and started to groan. . . . The hand over his mouth brought him awake instantly.

Fred's whisper was hot in his ear. "Someone coming. . . ." He was up, a Colt in his hand. McLain tossed aside his blanket and reached for his rifle. The wind barely stirred in the cottonwoods, and through the thin branches he could see the stars.

He heard the horse snort out past the spring . . . down by the old hotel. He padded after Fred. They hung back on the edge of the shadows. They could see the length of Tallow's palely lighted street. A horse waited with drooping head at the tie-bar of the old Reynolds House.

The rider was either drunk or hurt. He lay slumped over the horn, not stirring even when the tired animal blew again.

Fred looked at McLain. "Looks like —"

And Sandy nodded. "It's him — Rawlins!"

He handed Fred the rifle and walked toward the animal. Mel heard him. He raised his head. His face was a bloody mess. He said thickly: "McLain?"

Sandy trotted forward. "Yeah — it's me." Then he whirled, went into a crouch, his eyes searching the doorway of the abandoned house.

Rawlins called: "Chief! He's a friend!"

McLain sighed as the Navajo came out of the shadows. The Indian came to a halt by the mare, jerked a thumb toward the spring where Fred waited. His voice was a guttural command. "Tell partner come out, too."

McLain grinned. "Fred! The Chief's got you spotted."

Rawlins was making a terrible effort to sit up straight. "Ran into — trouble. Brother — Hump —"

Sandy cut him off. "It can wait, Mel. We'll take a look at that —" He caught Rawlins as he fell.

The Chief helped him free Mel's foot from his stirrup. "I take him," he said. "Strong Arm my friend."

Sandy relinquished Mel's limp form. Fred came running up; he made a grimace at the blood on Mel's features. "Reckon I

165

better get our medical supplies from my bag, Sandy."

McLain nodded. He turned to the Navajo, standing patiently with Mel's body. "Bring him in the house, Chief. We'll see what we can do for him."

Daylight was a gray smudge against the glassless windows of the old Reynolds House when Sandy brought in the first cup of coffee. Mel was sitting up. The bandage around his head made his face look black by contrast.

He took the cup and found the coffee too hot to drink. He walked to the lobby window, a tall, restless man with a slight limp caused by a bad gash on his left knee. There were coral rock cuts on the palms of his hands.

"Hump never was a good shot," he said. His voice was bitter. "I don't remember hitting the water. I floated around some and banged into some rocks. I didn't feel the cuts; not even the pain in my head. I don't know how long I was in the water . . . it seemed a heck of a long time. Then someone hauled me out. That's when I passed out."

He looked at the stolid Navajo. "The Chief told me he had followed me. He saw my brother get shot, too, right after I went over the cliff." He paused to gulp some coffee.

"The Chief says I kept saying Tallow — kept insisting I had to get here. So he packed me aboard the horse my brother had tied on the point, and we came here."

"Lucky thing for you," Sandy muttered. "You must live clean, Mel. That cut on your head ain't bad at all, but it shore looked like fury last night." He pointed outdoors. "Fred's cooking up some grub. You feel well enough to walk?"

"I'm well enough to ride," Mel growled.

"Ride?"

"Hump's dead," Mel said. "So is Bob. But the men who killed them are still loose. Carl told me about a desert camp. Said the boss had gone there to make arrangements for the new bunch that was being unloaded from the Hurricane. I know now he didn't think I'd live long enough to make use of the information. But there's a camp somewhere in the hills north of us —"

"Me know where to find camp," the Navajo said.

They looked at him. "Where?"

"Not too far. Long time me come from Navajo country. Come across desert.

Follow Apache trail —" He made a sweeping gesture. "Water in desert. River in canyon — comes and goes." His vocabulary was limited, but he managed by his expressions and gestures to get his meaning across. "Ol' Injun village in canyon."

"A village in the desert?" Sandy was shaking his head.

The Navajo nodded. "Injun people build um, long time ago. Then — pffft!" He shrugged. "Mebbe trouble come. Mebbe evil spirits. People go — no come back. Leave village."

"It might be the place," Mel muttered. "Can you take us there, Chief?"

The Navajo grunted.

"Wait a minute," Sandy protested. "We've only got three horses. The Chief'll have to walk."

"Me walk heap fast," the Navajo growled. "But eat first." He looked at Sandy slyly. "You have firewater?"

"Some," McLain admitted.

The Indian wiped his mouth with his hand. "Firewater heap good — make Chief remember old Apache trail —"

"Come on," Sandy snapped. "Let's eat first."

The Chief was making good his boast.

He set a steady jogging pace that brought grudging admiration from the three men riding behind him. Only once did he pause longer than a moment. He seemed puzzled for a while, until some landmark set him straight.

The sun was straight overhead, punishing the land with brutal heat, when the Chief halted. His shirt was dark with sweat. "Leave horses here," he directed.

Mel dismounted. His head felt light, and there was a dull ache behind his eyes. Sandy slid his rifle from the scabbard. Fred took the field glasses from Sandy's pack and followed the Chief up a rocky slope.

The Navajo got down on his stomach and crawled the remaining distance to the top. The others followed.

When they reached him, he pointed to something below. "Old village."

Mel squinted against the glare. Below, against the far canyon wall, were a number of square adobe cubicles, startlingly bright in the midday sun. They were piled one atop the other, as though they were toy building blocks. Pole ladders led from the ground to the roofs of the lower blocks, and other ladders on the roofs led up to the cubicles piled upon the base blocks. There were neither windows nor doors visible in these dwellings; all exits and entrances were through the same holes in the roofs.

Mel took the glasses Fred held out. Along the canyon floor a stream ran clear and shallow and vanished against the base of the red cliffs. Here and there among the cottonwoods and willows lining the stream, cattle grazed. Mel could make out horses among them . . . and one, a big blue roan standing clear of the trees, he recognized.

He knew, without being able to read the brand on the cattle, that Stirrup's beef was here.

He moved the glasses slowly along the stream and suddenly stopped. A whistle broke from him.

"Chinamen!"

Sandy took the glasses from him. "About half a dozen," he muttered. "Probably the sick ones who couldn't make the trip north across the desert with the original bunch. Sure," he said, turning to Mel. "That's why they smashed Stirrup. They didn't want anyone interfering with the wagons heading north."

Mel licked his dry lips. "Take another look, Sandy. Not countin' the Chinese, I make out only three men."

Sandy made a careful sweep of the canyon. "If there are others, they're well hidden.

Three's all I see, too. And from the looks of things they ain't expecting company."

"Let's treat them to a surprise," Mel said. He was smiling grimly as he pulled back from the rim.

Ed Walker, the heavy-set, bearded man who had been left in charge of the canyon hideout, walked over to the pail for a drink of water. The two yellow-skinned men who were sitting docilely in the scant shade cast by the covered wagon scrambled to their feet as he neared. Walker sneered. He was a naturally cruel man, and with Tane and the others gone, he had indulged in a cat-and-mouse game with these frightened, bewildered aliens until they jumped at the sight of him.

They had six of them in camp. Tane had gone back with Skinner and Keefer to pick up another load due in tonight.

Walker bent over the water pail and picked up the tin scoop. He was thinking that it was his turn tomorrow to ferry a wagonload of these frightened aliens to Johnson City, where a Chinese go-between would take them off his hands. Where the unlucky Chinamen went from there no longer concerned him.

He lifted the scoop and gargled dust

from his throat. A few feet away a poker-faced Chinese was stirring in a stew pan.

Walker spat out the water. He was tired of hanging around camp. And he didn't get along with the two others Tane had left there.

"Joe!" He called the man with a grating insolence that suggested trouble.

Joe looked up. He and the other man, Lefty Bowers, were brothers, slim, hard-faced men scarcely out of their teens. They had stretched a blanket between the two wagons and were playing pinochle. No one used the dark, musty dwellings. All of them, including the Chinese, preferred to live and sleep in the open.

"Joe!" Walker's tone was ugly.

Joe tossed his cards aside and got up. "Want something?" His voice was curt.

Walker scowled. "Yeah. I want you to ride up to the rim an' keep a lookout. Tane said there's a Border Patrol hombre been askin' questions in Manoas —"

"You stand guard in that hot sun!" Joe said coldly. "Darned if I will!" He sat down across from his brother and picked up his cards.

Walker cursed. In a sudden raging anger, he kicked the water pail, sending it clattering against the wagon wheel. It startled the Chinese standing over the stew, and in his terror he spilled the pot.

Walker turned on him, his anger finding an outlet in this harmless, terrified man. "You clumsy, lemon-hided son of Heaven! I'll teach you to spoil good chow!"

His gun jumped in his hand, and the Oriental screamed as he lifted his hand to his right ear, torn by the bullet. "Stand still!" Walker snarled. "Or by the eternal, you'll get the next slug between them slant eyes!"

"Leave the Chink alone!" Joe yelled, standing up. "He's worth money alive — not dead!"

Walker whirled. His face was hot and tight, and he felt ugly and confident with a gun in his hand. "You keep out of this! When I want you to horn in I'll whistle!"

Someone whistled from among the cottonwoods bordering the stream two hundred yards from the wagons. Then a voice, bright and cheerful, asked: "That good enough for you? Or do you want it louder?"

Walker whirled. Joe spun around and ran for his rifle, propped against the adobe wall twenty feet away. Lefty was scrambling to his feet.

The rifle from the willows spat a warning, the slug kicking up a spurt of dust between Joe and his rifle. The slim outlaw kept running, and the next bullet knocked him off his feet. He rolled over and started to crawl toward the rifle, a stubborn set to his pain-twisted mouth. The hidden rifleman broke his left arm. Joe decided to call it quits then.

Lefty had gained his feet. He had drawn his Colt, but he couldn't see anyone to use it on, and he didn't dare make a break, after seeing what had happened to his brother.

But Walker, closer to one of the wagons, took a chance.

He reached the bleeding Chinese in one jump, whirled him around in front of himself to shield himself from the rifleman. Then he shoved the man sprawling across the fire and broke toward the end of the wagon. The rifle slug took three inches of shirt and skin from his right shoulder. But he made the back of the wagon, skidded around and fired at the wiry figure he saw running along the adobe buildings.

His shot spun Fred Humes around. The lawman managed to hobble back around the corner and disappeared.

Walker pressed back against the tailgate,

a trapped expression on his bearded face. He heard a cold voice call: "This way, Mac," and jerked around to face Mel Rawlins. He didn't know Mel by name — he saw only a tall, easy-striding man with a bandaged head, and he cut up and fired hastily.

Mel drove him back with a slug in the shoulder. Walker lurched around the wagon and ran head on into a rifle slug. He slewed around and fell across the spilled stew and lay there.

Mel walked toward Lefty, who had dropped his Colt as though it were a hot coal. He waved toward the willows. Sandy McLain stepped out, holding his rifle.

Mel turned to Lefty. "Where are the others?"

Lefty bit his lip. "Which others?"

Mel lifted the muzzle of his Colt and thumbed back the hammer. "Let's try it again, feller. Where's Tane?"

Lefty began to sweat. "Tane drove the wagon to the coast," he mumbled. "Skinner an' Keefer went with him."

"To Cauldron Point?"

Lefty looked surprised. "How'd you know?"

Mel ignored him. He knew now he had to get back to Manoas. The Hurricane was coming in off the point tonight.

Sandy said: "Looks like Fred got a slug in his right leg. The Indian's with him —"

"We're through here," Mel said. "I'm going back to Manoas."

Sandy turned. "Not without me, you don't. Fred an' the Navajo can take care of things here. They can drive back to town in one of the wagons."

Mel shrugged. "If you think you can leave your partner — ?"

"He wouldn't want it any other way," Sandy said grimly. "Don't forget, Mel — this is my job, too!"

Chapter XV

The fog rolled in all along the coast that night. It was a thin haze at first, moving slowly, like a gray mist off the face of the sea. Gradually the headlands grew blurred and the lights of Manoas shone faintly through the murk.

The Hurricane slid through the fog, sails half furled. She ran like a dark shadow through the night, the oil calm water hissing softly along her sides. Captain Bremem hunched over the wheel and peered through the gray soup, guided by the lights of the town.

His first mate, Lafe Tulafson, a dour-faced Swede with huge-knuckled hands, came to the bridge. "They'll be waiting for us, Captain, at Cauldron Point."

"Let them wait!" Bremem snarled. "I've got a little business of my own tonight!"

Lafe shrugged. "Aye, Captain."

The Hurricane came into the cove without her lights, a silent shadow. They dropped anchor without a splash.

Five minutes later Captain Bremem and Lafe went over the side to a waiting dinghy where a seaman, already at the oars, waited. The man bent to his task as Lafe pushed away from the anchored schooner.

They tied up at the jetty, the seaman remaining by the small boat. From the pier, the Hurricane was barely visible.

Bremem and his first mate went up the steep slope to the Sea Horse. Bremem kept his hand in the pocket of his short coat, fingers gripped tight about the trigger guard of a snub-nosed .38.

The notes of a score written by a long dead composer came out to them as they paused in front of the Sea Horse. Captain Bremem smiled — not from appreciation, for he had no ear for this kind of music, but because it told him that Loan Stevens was inside.

Tobey was behind his bar, leaning over the counter. He was working on his ledger, a small frown of concentration on his face. He heard the doors creak, and he looked up, and surprise flashed across his features.

Loan stopped playing. She swiveled around and watched Captain Bremem and his first mate head for the bar.

Tobey said: "Captain! I thought you

were —" He shot a quick look at Loan.

"Due at the point?" Bremem laughed. "There's all night, Tobey — all night." He kept his right hand in his pocket and pounded on the bar with the other.

"You treating us tonight?"

Tobey's jaw took on a grim slant. But he kept his temper. "Sure." He turned and took a bottle from the shelf behind him and put two glasses on the bar. "Thought you'd be halfway to Tampico by now —"

"Like fun you did!" Bremem said. His voice had a nasty edge. "I been anchored ten miles out for three days, Tobey, and you know it!"

Tobey's teeth gritted. "You fool! What do you want — ?"

"Money. All I've got coming. Right now."

Tobey shook his head. Loan was coming toward them, her face troubled.

"I told you I'd settle things later, after you unload —"

Bremem took his hand out of his pocket and rested the muzzle of the .38 on the edge of the bar. "Right now!" His voice was ugly.

Loan came up swiftly. "Tobey! What's he back for? What does he want?"

Bremem caught her by the arm and spun

her around to Lafe. "Hold her!"

The girl screamed. Lafe clapped a huge hand over her mouth. She tried to squirm free, tried to kick him. He held her with stolid indifference.

Tobey's voice shook. "You fool! You gone crazy, Bremem? I told you I'd pay you when you came back!"

Bremem's shot grazed Tobey's cheek. The tall New Englander stood still, his face like stone. Blood made a tiny trickle down his face.

"Now!" Bremem rasped.

Tobey nodded. "Let Loan go. I'll get the money."

Bremem shook his head. "That's something else I've come back for, Tobey. For her." He was a burly figure, in complete control of things. "You told me you'd never let any man have her! But I'm taking her, Tobey! And the devil with you!"

Tobey's voice seemed smothered by a deep, futile rage. "You crazy fool! Do you think you can get away with a thing like that?"

"The sea leaves no trail!" Bremem reminded him.

Loan had ceased struggling. Her eyes were on Tobey in mute appeal. Tobey nodded. "I've got the money, Bremem.

180

Right here —" He ducked behind the counter for the Colt he kept on the shelf and made a good try.

Bremem's bullet knocked him back against the shelves, and his shot went up through the ceiling. Bremem's second shot slid him down out of sight.

Loan squirmed free. She screamed once and ran for the door. Bremem whirled. He intercepted her, and she turned on him, clawing at his face. He shoved his gun into his pocket, tried to pin her arms. Her nails drew blood down his cheek, and he lost his temper. He brought his fist down in a slashing blow across her jaw.

Loan's eyes glazed. Her knees buckled, and Bremem caught her. He held her until Lafe reached them. The first mate swung her limp body across his shoulder and turned toward the door.

Neither the gunshots nor the girl's screams brought anyone to the Sea Horse. Bremem had his fingers around the pistol as he opened the door.

He looked out and saw nothing but a gray mist. "All clear," he growled.

Walking quickly, they disappeared into the fog. Loan regained consciousness as Lafe was passing her down to the oarsman in the dinghy. By the time she realized where she was, the small boat was free of the jetty, heading into the gray murk.

The Hurricane was no longer visible. Bremem cupped his hands to his mouth and gave a cautious: "Ahoy, Hurricane!"

A voice answered at once, from off to the right. The oarsman corrected his direction. The guiding voice sounded every few moments, until the dinghy bumped softly against the Hurricane's hull.

A dark shape loomed over the ladder. Lafe went up first. Bremem took Loan's arm and forced her to her feet. "You better climb," he advised her harshly.

On deck, Bremem turned to Lafe. "Lock her in my cabin. We're headed for Cauldron Point. We'll get rid of the Chinks and come back for our money. . . ."

Ten minutes later the Hurricane left the cove, swinging wide of the hidden headland, sliding like a gray ghost through the fog.

The sea mist thickened, piling up in soft gray layers over the town of Manoas. Manassas Smith stood in his stocking feet, staring up toward the lights of the Sea Horse. The fog had brought misery to his old bones, and he had been rubbing himself with horse linament when he'd heard the shots. He was normally a curious man, but he was a cautious man, too, which accounted for his untroubled existence in Manoas.

By the time he had pulled on a coat and reached the street, Bremem and Lafe, carrying the girl, had already passed and been swallowed up by the fog piling in from the sea.

For a few moments Smith was torn between curiosity and prudence. Eventually curiosity won out.

Tobey Hawkins was just coming to his feet behind the bar when Smith entered. He threw a wild look at the small man, then ignored him. He had a Colt in his hand. He lurched along the bar and reached the far end and leaned over it, his breathing coming in short gasping gulps. A dark stain was spreading above his belt buckle.

Smith watched, fascinated. The man was hit hard. But Tobey Hawkins was just coming to his feet behind the at the gun in his fist, threw it away.

He turned and made his way back to where the old harpoon lay on pegs. He took it down. The barbed iron tip reflected the lamplight as he came around the bar and headed for the door.

Smith stepped aside. Tobey reeled past him and went out. He headed down the steep road, a strange, lurching figure with a weapon seldom seen in that country.

Smith followed at a discreet distance.

The owner of the Sea Horse pounded on the door of one of the fishing shacks lining the shore. After a moment the door opened. Lamplight made a streak against the mist.

"Corrado! I want a boat and two good men, now!" Tobey's voice was startlingly clear, carrying to Smith.

Corrado went back into the shack, and a moment later he and a younger man joined Tobey. Smith went no further. He watched them vanish toward the water. The sounds of a boat being pushed across gravel to the surf, of oars being fitted to oarlocks, were remarkably clear, as though the fog amplified all noise.

The small boat pulled away from the beach and was lost in the mist. The sound of rowing faded slowly into the night.

Chapter XVI

As Mel Rawlins and McLain rode into Manoas, the fog was clammy against their faces. The mist, rolling inland, had caught them in the back hills, so that only luck had guided them to this coast town — the chance glimpse of a feeble light in the grayness that stretched like an endless sea ahead of them.

They came down off the ridge, and Mel headed directly for the Sea Horse. A small man loomed up out of the haze as they dismounted, and Mel whirled, a Colt sliding into his fist.

Smith shrank back, his voice quick. "What in tarnation's going on tonight?"

"Smith?" Sandy turned to the man.

"It's me," the stableman growled. "What're you two doing in town tonight?"

Mel ignored him. He went into the Sea Horse and pulled up at the bar. His voice was harsh in the stillness. "Tobey!"

Smith answered him. "He's gone out. I

think Loan's gone, too." He came into the room with Sandy.

"Heard shots. Thought I heard a girl scream, too. When I got here Tobey was just getting up. He was in bad shape. But he took that old harpoon of his and headed for the beach. . . ."

Mel looked at Sandy. "Bremem came back. Came here first."

"Only one thing would keep Tobey going tonight," Smith said: "Loan Stevens." He shook his head. "He's headed for Cauldron Point in a small boat, an' he's carryin' a harpoon. I hope he makes it in time."

Mel turned on his heel. "We'll make it first, Sandy. I know the way!"

The going was slow over the ridge. The horses felt their way, snorting fearfully. There was little to go by. Then somewhere off to the right, in the gray blackness, a foghorn tooted.

Mel and Sandy dismounted. They could follow the trail better this way. When they came to a small draw behind the point, they left the horses.

The foghorn tooted again, querulously.

They made the beach below. The waves slithered on the coarse sand. Sandy's fingers suddenly gripped Mel's arm.

Off somewhere to the right a peevish voice said: "Why don't the fools come in?"

Mel nodded. He and Sandy eased through the fog. Ahead of them, drawn up close to the water, a covered wagon loomed up. They could barely make out a figure on the seat, smoking. A man was standing by the horses, a rifle in his hands.

A voice from the tailgate halted Mel. "Where's Tobey?" The figure moved into sight, holding a lantern. He was a thin, reedy individual with a nasal drawl. "The boss is always on hand when we load up."

From up front Tane's voice said: "He'll be here. You're gettin' jittery as an old woman, Skinner!"

The man by the horses put in his two cents' worth. "Count me in with Skinner, Tane. I don't like this fog. An' I don't trust that crew on the Hurricane."

Tane was disgusted. "I should have left you and Skinner back at camp. Walker would have jumped at the chance to come along."

"Walker's a fool!" Keefer growled. He jerked his rifle up as a sound came out of the darkness. It was an oarlock being rattled.

"Give them the light," Tane growled.

Out of the dark sea the Hurricane hooted cautiously.

Skinner held up the lantern, lowered it, raised it, lowered it again.

Out on the water a light flashed red, winked yellow, flashed red. Then it disappeared.

"They saw us," Tane said. "Put the lantern back and come up here. I want to stretch my legs."

Skinner grunted. He headed for the back of the wagon and didn't see the gun butt that slammed against his ear. He fell against the tailgate, and the horses up front jerked.

Tane yelled: "Watch that lantern, you fool!"

Mel handed the lantern to Sandy and climbed in over the tailgate. The wagon was empty. Two wooden benches lined the sides. He could see Tane's head and shoulders up front.

He moved cautiously toward the man.

Tane turned. "What's holdin' you, Skinner?" His voice was impatient.

He saw Mel loom up, and the white bandage warned him. He tried to jump clear. Mel's fingers closed on his collar and hauled him back. Tane twisted, fumbling for his gun. "Keefer —"

Mel slammed his Colt down. Tane was trying to break loose, and the barrel came

188

down across his cheek, ripping a deep gash. He started to cry out, and Mel's steely fingers closed around his throat. He brought his Colt down again, hard.

Tane slumped back, and Mel hauled him into the wagon.

Keefer was staring at the seat in paralyzed wonder. He heard a boot scrape on a wet rock behind him and turned. His rifle blasted a wild shot skyward just as Sandy McLain rammed his shoulder into the man. Keefer fell heavily over a slick rock, and McLain came down hard with both knees on the man's chest. The breath whooshed out of Keefer.

He turned and looked up at Mel as Rawlins stepped across the wagon seat.

Out on the dark water, the sound of oarlocks was coming closer.

Mel jumped down and helped Sandy haul Keefer into the wagon beside Tane. "I'll take Tane's place," he whispered.

Sandy nodded. He pressed back against the tailgate and listened to the sound of the approaching boat.

Mel climbed up into the wagon seat and pulled his hat down over his eyes. The bandage barely showed.

Moments later a small boat loomed out of the grayness. Mel could make out a man standing in the bow, holding a lantern in his hand. He was a big, raw-boned figure wearing a mate's cap. A smaller man toiled at the oars. Five small figures were huddled in the stern.

The boat grated on sand, and the man with the lantern jumped out and hauled the skiff up on the beach. He didn't wait for the others. He came toward the wagon, swinging the lantern.

"Got twenty for you this trip," he said. "Five here, and fifteen more aboard."

Mel waited. The others were coming up behind the man with the lantern. One was a chunky seaman. The rest were frightened Chinese.

"Heard a shot," Lafe said, holding up the lantern so as to take a look at Mel. "Any trouble?"

"No," Mel answered. "We thought you didn't see us. Skinner got nervous."

"Oh?" Lafe peered up at him. "Hey, you're not Tane!"

He turned to run. Mel jumped down from the seat. Lafe plunged into the group of Chinese, and they went down in a sprawling tangle. When he tried to get up, Mel's boot pressed down hard on his neck.

"Act peaceful," Mel growled, "or you'll get hurt!"

He took his foot away, and Lafe came to his feet. Sandy was coming toward them, the rifle in his hands acting as a pacifier. The seaman was holding his hands high, a startled look on his face.

Lafe shot a look out over the water. In the shrouding fog, the Hurricane tooted a puzzled blast.

Mel said: "Get into the wagon. The Chinese, too."

Lafe complied. He helped load Skinner's unconscious form over the tailgate and crawled in. The Chinese huddled on the beach around the boat, looking frightened.

Mel said: "This is my show, Sandy. You keep an eye on these hombres. I'm going aboard the Hurricane."

Sandy started to protest, but realized that one of them had to stay. He shrugged. "Wish you luck, Mel!"

Rawlins prodded the sullen seaman with the muzzle of his Colt. "You'll row me back. And you'll keep your mouth shut!"

They left the puzzled Chinese on the beach. Mel stepped into the stern, and the seaman pushed the skiff off the sand and stepped inside. Sullenly he took up the oars and began to row.

Chapter XVII

Out on that fog-shrouded sea a boat probed, manned by two heavy-shouldered Mexican fishermen. Tobey sat in the bow of the small craft, his knees spread wide. The harpoon lay across them. His face was as white as paper.

Corrado paused in his rowing, listening. Tobey's harsh whisper ordered him: "Keep rowing!"

They moved through a silent world. Long familiarity with this rugged coast guided Corrado and his son. They paused again, listening to the sound of the waves breaking against the rocks, and though they couldn't see the shoreline, Corrado said: "Cauldron Point, *Señor* Tobey."

Tobey nodded. He was getting weaker, and his face had a ghastly look. "Hurry!"

The fishermen resumed rowing. A few moments later Tobey grinned crookedly as the Hurricane's foghorn sounded, locating the hidden ship for them. The oarsmen slowed, barely dipping their oars into the dark water.

The Hurricane took shape up ahead, a long, low silhouette against the mist.

Tobey made a motion, and the fishermen drew in their oars. The boat drifted toward the seaward side of the anchored vessel. It slid in under the Hurricane's bow, and Tobey caught a trailing line and held the boat in close against the ship's side.

Corrado's son held Tobey's harpoon as his father boosted the ex-whaler up to the low railing. A moment later Tobey reached down and took the harpoon from him.

Corrado cast off. From the shore a skiff was making its way toward the Hurricane. The fishermen who had brought Tobey looked at one another as they headed back for the cove at Manoas.

Tobey crouched among the coils of rope and gear at the bow, orienting himself. Midway down the shoreward rail, illumined by a lantern hung on the mast, a cluster of men formed a dark, waiting group.

Tobey hefted the harpoon. It had been a long time since he had used it, and never on a man. But tonight he was going to kill Captain Bremem with it!

The captain was standing by the rope ladder, while just beyond two crewmen, flanked by a group of shivering Chinese, were watching for the approaching skiff. The captain was plainly nervous.

"Call again," he directed one of the crewmen. "If Lafe doesn't answer, we'll up anchor. I don't like the feel of this. I'm not waiting to —"

"You've waited too long already, Captain!" Tobey's voice was as bleak as death.

Bremem whirled. He saw the tall figure coming at him from the bow, the man he thought he had killed in the Sea Horse. Fear held him rigid against the low railing. Then he remembered the gun in his pocket and jammed his hand in after it.

He saw the harpoon come up, and he gave a strangled cry as he tried to turn away from it.

The harpoon's barbed point entered Bremem's side just below his left armpit, splintering ribs, driving cleanly through him. Bremem's outcry was choked off. The force of the harpoon drive knocked him off balance. He fell against the railing and toppled over. His body made a loud splash.

Tobey waited in the shadows, swaying a little. But his voice held a harsh ring of authority.

"Where's Miss Stevens?"

One of the men standing by the Chinese said, "Down in the captain's cabin, Tobey. I'll go get her."

He ducked down the ladder. Tobey's knees buckled and he lurched toward the railing. He put his hands down to steady himself.

Down by the rope ladder, a skiff bumped against the Hurricane's side. Tobey braced himself.

A tall, lean figure came up over the side. He jumped clear and whirled, his Colt holding Tobey and the small group beyond. There was enough light for him to recognize Tobey.

"Got here — a little late," Tobey said. His voice was forced. "I've been expecting you."

"Where's Captain Bremem?"

"In — Davey Jones' locker." Tobey raised his hands slowly. "Put that gun away, Mel. I've played my last hand."

He eased back against the railing. "Hardest man to kill I ever saw," he said. "Got nine lives — like a cat —"

"You killed Hump?" Mel's voice was curious. "You kill Bob, too?"

Tobey nodded. "No hard feelings. They — were in the way. Had a good thing here. Captain Bremem brought the Chinks in. I smuggled them — across the desert. Lot of money in it — enough for me and Loan — some day —"

A spasm went through him. He turned and slid along the railing and fell hard. He gasped once before he died.

Loan's voice reached Mel and caused him to turn around. She was standing by the hatch, a small, disheveled figure with an ugly bruise under her eye.

"I heard him, Mel. I heard him. . . ." She came to Rawlins, crying.

The fog lifted in the morning, and the Hurricane's crew took the schooner around the point, into the cove at Manoas. Mel and Loan went ashore. Mel helped Sandy take charge of the prisoners, herding them into a storeroom in the Sea Horse.

The law from Idalgo County showed up later in the day. Fred Humes and the Chief had taken their wagon to the county seat and told the law there about Manoas.

Sandy shook hands with Mel before he left. "Fred'll be laid up for a while with a game leg," he said slyly. "Need a good partner. If you're free . . . ?"

Mel shook his head. "I never was easy

with the law, remember?" He looked at Loan. They were in the Sea Horse, where Loan had been packing her things.

"I've got other plans, Sandy."

They walked out to the porch with the lawman. The Hurricane lay at anchor under a blue sky.

Loan said: "I wonder what they'll do with her."

Mel shrugged. "I don't care. I've had enough of the sea . . ." He was thinking of Stirrup, and of what he would have to tell his mother and Ruth.

It was a problem he would have to face. The telling — and the rebuilding of Stirrup.

The cross atop the mission glinted in the sun. He took Loan's arm. "I think we can get Father Pinone to marry us," he said. "That is, if you're willing."

Loan moved close, smiling. "It's the thing to do, Mel — before going home!"